"Did you want some help?"

His eyes glued themselves to the patch of skin above her panties, where her hand toyed with the shirt hem.

Damn. Her.

How could Shannon play games like this when their split had nearly killed him?

"No, thanks," he said, turning back to the make-shift shelter he was setting up. Seeing Shannon undressed had the power to make him stupid.

"Then I'll just take my pilfered hotel soap and find someplace private to put this rainfall to work." She waved a tiny white bar she must have picked up at the resort.

"Shannon?" he called as she started to walk away.

She turned, her wet hair sliding against her shoulder as she looked at him expectantly.

"You know you're killing me, don't you?"

Her sole response was a smile, before she and her pink panties disappeared into the darkness....

Blaze

Dear Reader,

There's something sexy about a rock 'n roll hero. I think we love our musicians because they are a new incarnation of the poet/troubadour. Their lyrics touch our hearts and speak to our experiences, setting our lives to song. And at the most basic level, what woman doesn't approve of the man who can move her hips?

For this book I decided to look beyond that cool rocker facade to the man beneath and see what it might be like to fall in love with a guy who is in the public eye. A guy women around the globe vie for. Of course, the story got a little more complicated when I gave my rocker a heroine who was every bit as in demand as him.

I hope you enjoy Shannon and Romero's journey. And the next time your own life journey takes an unexpected turn, keep in mind that sometimes being lost is the only way to find yourself.

Happy reading,

Joanne Rock

She Thinks Her Ex Is Sexy...

JOANNE ROCK

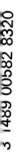
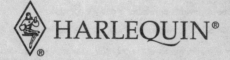

HARLEQUIN®

TORONTO • NEW YORK • LONDON
AMSTERDAM • PARIS • SYDNEY • HAMBURG
STOCKHOLM • ATHENS • TOKYO • MILAN • MADRID
PRAGUE • WARSAW • BUDAPEST • AUCKLAND

Recycling programs
for this product may
not exist in your area.

ISBN-13: 978-0-373-79454-6
ISBN-10:   0-373-79454-1

SHE THINKS HER EX IS SEXY...

Copyright © 2009 by Joanne Rock.

ABOUT THE AUTHOR

Three-time RITA® Award nominee and Golden Heart winner Joanne Rock is the author of more than thirty novels for Harlequin Books. She is fascinated by what draws people together, and she finds inspiration for her books while studying Myers-Briggs profiles, astrology charts, Enneagrams and the occasional personal ad. Whether she is writing a medieval historical or a sexy contemporary story, she enjoys exploring the dynamics that create a lasting relationship. Learn more about Joanne and her work by visiting her at joannerock.com or at myspace.com/joanne_rock.

Books by Joanne Rock

To Arianna Hart, who adores those rocker
heroes the same way I do.

Thanks for being such a fabulous friend!

1

"EVERY SINGLE PERSON in this hotel is getting it on right now except me." Shannon Leigh cradled her cell phone against one shoulder as she packed her suitcase in the exclusive Mexican seaside resort, her emotions in more disarray than her stale career. "It's like the Cupid wedding theme ran wild and infected every employee and guest in the place. I just went to hunt down more towels, and even the maid is getting busy in the supply closet."

"Eeeww." Shannon's agent, Ceily, was back home in L.A. She started her day at 6:00 a.m. so Shannon hadn't felt terribly guilty about waking her at five to share the trauma of this Valentine weekend wedding from hell.

Shannon's best friend had gotten married in a romantic private ceremony in La Paz on the Baja Peninsula and Shannon had been the maid of honor. Too bad she'd agreed to the Cupid fest before the best man—her rock-star boyfriend of almost a year—had broken up with her. She'd been stuck watching him charm his way through the wedding, with adoring female guests throwing themselves at his feet wherever he went. She'd been due to finally escape the night before—until her charter flight had been canceled because of engine trouble. A situation Romero had heard about during the reception, promptly and publicly offering to drive her back to L.A. the following morning.

Now technically today.

How could she have refused gracefully without drawing more attention to a breakup that still had the tabloids buzzing three months after the fact?

Shannon had no idea how she would survive the long trip ensconced in a small sports car with one of the sexiest men in the known universe. And that wasn't just her opinion. Look up any poll on hot rockers and Romero Jinks topped the charts. She just wanted to get the hell out of the sex-drenched hotel and back to real life. Back to salvaging her imperiled career.

"Tell me about it. I was trying diligently to avoid any more romance references after the overexposure to pink roses, pink champagne and pink bridesmaid dresses. Then I have to stumble into a storage-room orgy." She yanked the lemon-yellow dress she'd worn to the rehearsal dinner from the closet and tossed it onto the bed, trying not to think about how long it had been since she'd had sex. Three months without Romero had been—lonely. But even before that there'd been the fights and the nights alone in his king-size bed while he made love to his damn guitar instead of her.

Their relationship had been deteriorating for months from lack of communication and—often—lack of presence on the same continent. She'd needed to talk and connect with him, while he preferred long stretches of brooding alone time that fueled his music and left her frustrated. The whole precarious situation had imploded over the stupidest fight ever when he'd bought new hiking boots for his entire entourage but hadn't bothered to toss a pair in her direction.

She'd been petty to erupt about something so superficial, but it wasn't about the damn boots. She'd been tired of being a nonentity to him, while he'd meant so much to her.

"You should totally report her, and I don't want you using those towels." Ceily's voice cracked, no doubt because she hadn't had her morning coffee or her first cigarette of the day, which, bizarrely, seemed to clear her throat.

Shannon's high-heeled slipper caught in the strap of her sequined bag and she tripped, twisting her ankle. And shouldn't she know better than to march around the room in a snit? How many times had she cringed as a kid when her mother threw tantrums?

"Damn it!" She cursed the satin-and-rhinestone slippers and kicked them both off, sending them sliding along the terrazzo floor covered with Navajo rugs. "I can't report her because I didn't actually catch her boinking the night manager. I just saw her blouse all wrinkled and her hair undone while he pretended to look around a ten-by-ten storage room for his clipboard."

She threw the sequined bag into her vintage canvas luggage and rubbed her leg, not giving Ceily time to comment before another thought occurred to her.

"Come to think of it, their act to cover up what they'd been doing was so good, you should be sending *them* on casting calls instead of me." Her ankle throbbed, but not nearly as much as her heart aching at the thought of her career in a downward spiral along with her romantic life.

She'd received no serious offers for roles after her last part in a "B" thriller, a sure sign she was closing in on the end of her marginal profession as an actress. She had a backup plan to move to New York and try theater, but that hadn't been her dream when she'd watched her movie-star mother throw away her own career to drug addiction and bad choices.

Shannon had always thought she'd be able to mold a stronger, healthier path through Tinseltown than her mom, but after almost fifteen years of effort, she hadn't even come close to Bridget Leigh's fame. Still, she wouldn't be so blue about any of it if the career news hadn't come so hot on the heels of her breakup.

This weekend sure had rubbed Shannon's nose in all of her failures. Her best friend had made her trip down the aisle the day before, even though Shannon had spent *twice* as long in a committed relationship as Amy. While she was happy for her bud, Shannon's eleven-and-a-half-month stint with Romero had gone up in flames and it still hurt to be reminded of what she'd lost. She'd even had to close the French doors overlooking the ocean to drown out the chorus of orgasmic sighs drifting on the breeze.

Unfortunately, shutting the door didn't shut down the conviction that one of the orgasmic sighs came from the woman her guitar-playing ex-boyfriend had danced with three times at the reception.

"Shannon, I will find you a great part," Ceily assured her. "You're good at what you do and you're a professional. You know as well as I do how rare that is in this business."

"Rare like women over thirty?" Rising from the bed, she stuffed her pink bridesmaid dress into her suitcase, remembering how fantastic Romero had looked in his tuxedo on the beach the day before.

"Honey, tell that to Goldie Hawn."

"A glittering exception to the rule," Shannon grumbled, in no mood to be placated when her life in Hollywood was very possibly over. Why did Romero have to prod their limping relationship into gasping heart failure right when the rest of her world was coming apart? Especially since she'd been so careful to shield his artistically sensitive self from her problems so as not to disrupt his all-important songwriting. "Although I have no business dragging all my problems to your doorstep. I just wanted to tell you not to worry about the dogs today. I'll be home in time to feed Abbott and Costello tonight."

Assuming, of course, she made it back to L.A. and her two Pekingese-Chihuahua mixes without succumbing to the temptation to drag Romero off to a Mexican hideaway and remind him exactly how good they'd been together. A juvenile move that would feel great in the short run and only hurt more tomorrow. She'd made it three months without him, hadn't she?

She moved back to the closet and promptly stumbled on the slippers she'd tossed moments before. One pedicured toenail banged against a satin buckle on the discarded shoes and broke, tearing halfway across the nail bed. Pitching both slippers into the suitcase, where she should have put them in the first place, she hopped on one foot toward her purse to find a bandage for her injured ankle.

"Shanny, you don't need to apologize." Ceily's voice went maternal and soft, reminding Shannon of how many ways this woman had filled the void in her life after her superstar mother had overdosed. Shannon had been celebrating her fourteenth birthday with friends when her mom had taken too many sleeping pills. She'd never figured out if it had been intentional or not, but even after all the fights with her mother, Shannon missed her moments of clarity. When Bridget Leigh wasn't drugged up or foisting her own insecurities onto Shannon, she had been one of those bright light personalities that outshone anyone else in the room.

Shannon was clearing an unexpected lump from her throat when Ceily spoke again.

"Honey, since you've got that long ride home with your ex today, I wondered if you would ask him to call me? I met a producer who knows that I rep you, and he asked me about the possibility of getting Romero to play himself in a docudrama about his old band, Jinxed."

Shannon dropped the bandage she'd found, the white wrapper slipping back into the uncharted depths of a purse filled with everything from her BlackBerry to a twelve-piece makeup brush set. Shannon's current career choices consisted of a sleazy independent film about her actress mother's life or a role on the small-time theater circuit off Broadway, yet Romero didn't even need to pursue acting to find film roles.

"You want *me* to ask him?" Shannon couldn't help a quick mental image of herself pouring a pound of salt in the gaping wound of her chest. And, yeah, a bit of her ego smarted here, too. "Our careers became a bit of a sore subject for us, Ceily."

Part of it was because they couldn't find the right

balance of work and romance. Part of it was because she struggled to get ahead in her job while everything Romero touched turned to gold.

Or maybe that's just how she felt every time he touched her. Fortunate. Fantastic. Priceless.

And, oh, God, she couldn't stand the thought of him touching another woman when he'd been her man just three short months ago. From his killer dark eyes to the shoulder-length, silky black waves that would have done an eighties hair band proud, Romero was seriously hot. Even better, he wrote music that was soul deep and complex. His lyrics had seduced her long before the rest of him did.

"If you talk him into it, I'll slide you a finder's fee," Ceily offered while Shannon stared up at the tiled ceiling where a heavy mahogany ceiling fan spun on low speed.

Great. And Shannon could have a bit part in the "babes he'd banged" section of the docudrama. She yanked the headset off her ears to give it a shake.

"Given the way we broke up, I think I'm the last person he'll want to talk to about his career." There was a chance she'd been a smidge unreasonable about it in that final fight, telling him he always put his guitar before her. But she'd tried so hard to fit into his life for so long that all the frustrations she'd been stuffing down had bubbled up like red-hot, angry lava. "But for you, I'll at least mention it."

"Excellent. And from my memories of the two of you together, I'll bet he pays more attention to you than you realize." Ceily sighed with the dreaminess of someone who'd only seen the Shannon and Romero relationship from the outside. They'd fooled a lot of people into thinking they were wildly in love before the bottom fell out of a charade Shannon had nursed along out of pure wishful thinking.

She said goodbye to Ceily before hitting the disconnect button.

Ceily's false impression of Romero still caring tweaked Shannon's heart more than she would have liked after this long time apart from the man. And, coming on the heels of the sexual symphony in progress around her, the conversation hadn't exactly improved Shannon's mood. She'd really thought Romero could be the one, yet he'd looked as if the breakup was no big deal to him when he'd soaked up feminine admiration and the La Paz sunshine yesterday. He'd never given her reason to be jealous in the past, but she wasn't foolish enough to think he hadn't moved on. Women had always—would always—throw themselves at him.

Flopping down onto the pillow-top mattress with her hair wrapped in a towel full of deep conditioner, Shannon squeezed her eyes shut tight and prayed for the next twenty-four hours to be over with as fast as possible. Romero had told her to meet him at ten that morning, but she would be ready to leave in five minutes.

She just wanted to get back home so she could officially end this chapter of her life. Once she moved to New York, she would put her movie career and her too-sexy ex behind her for good.

"CAN'T YOU GO ANY FASTER?"

Romero Jinks tightened his grip on the steering wheel at his ex-girlfriend's latest request, in a litany that had started at nine o'clock that morning with a wake-up call asking him when he'd be ready to leave.

Who woke up at nine after a wedding reception that had lasted into the wee hours of the morning? But that was Shannon. An early bird, a night owl, and all around too much energy for him to keep up with. At thirty years old, she seemed impossibly young to him even though they were only eight years apart. Blond, blue-eyed and built like a fifties pinup girl, she was too sexy by half, but that was only a fraction of her appeal. He'd been drawn by her energy and enthusiasm when they'd first met. She'd been a spark to his creativity and his life, pulling him out of a long writing drought with her vibrancy. He'd been crazy about her until she'd blindsided him with a wealth of frustrations about their relationship, culminating in the stupidest argument he'd ever been a part of.

How many women picked a fight because their guy failed to purchase a pair of hiking boots for her? When he'd offered for them to spend some time apart until she cooled down, she'd promptly pulled his clothes out of the closet and boxed up everything he owned in an all-night packing craze. After almost a year together, she'd created a drama the whole neighborhood had witnessed as she'd methodically carried the crates out to the curb.

"I'm not going any faster." Romero checked the speedometer and slowed down—not to purposely piss her off, but because he was already doing eighty miles an hour up the Baja Peninsula to reach the California state line as soon as he could. The last thing he wanted was to extend their time in Mexico with a stint in a stink-hole prison cell.

They'd passed the last town, Insurgentes, long ago

in the hunt for a shortcut home. He was seriously tearing up his new car driving this fast on pavement that hadn't seen a road crew in a decade.

A small price to pay if it shortened the trip. Only a few more hours to go and they could split for good. No more saccharine sweet Valentine weddings to trap them back into pseudocouplehood. Playing the best man to her maid of honor, dancing that requisite dance with the woman who'd once meant everything to him, had been exquisite torture to a nerve that hadn't fully healed.

Of course, he couldn't blame this trip on anyone but himself, since he'd scrambled to offer her a ride when her flight had been canceled. He'd seen a chance to salvage her pride, knowing damn well her finances wouldn't support a last-minute ticket out of Mexico. At least not easily. Shannon had tried to hide her dwindling movie prospects from him, but he knew the last couple of parts she'd taken weren't worthy of her talents.

"Would you like me to drive?" She peered across the console of his new BMW coupe, a vehicle he'd picked up shortly before the Mexico trip. He'd ordered it months ago, thinking it would be fun to have for a trip up the coast to celebrate his first-year anniversary with Shannon.

An anniversary that never happened, thanks to her decision to launch World War Three. He'd postponed picking up the car, considering it now represented his failure. He'd been too blind to see what Shannon was feeling until she'd spelled it out in angry detail after it was too late.

"No, thanks." He figured the less said, the better. That strategy wouldn't make the time pass any quicker, though.

"What did you think of the ceremony?" she asked,

her fingers clutching the silver Celtic knot on a chain around her neck and raking the pendant back and forth across the tiny links.

She looked incredible in her tight jeans and purple satin shoes with high heels that just barely brought her to five foot eight. She wore a lavender cotton tank top with an ivory satin blazer that had big purple rhinestone buttons in the shape of flowers. A skinny silver scarf hung loose around her neck. The scarf didn't serve a great purpose now, but he'd seen her tie that sort of thing around her head like a hippie-chick bandanna, or a wrap for a ponytail if she wanted her hair out of her face.

She was a first-class Hollywood diva on the outside, but there'd been a time when he felt as if he knew her better than that—the down-to-earth woman she could be with him at home. He hadn't seen that side of her in a long while, but then again, he'd been on tour a lot. And he'd been in the music business long enough to know the people you cared about could change while you were out on the road. It wouldn't be the first time he'd left one woman and returned to—seemingly—someone else.

He just couldn't recall it ever bothering him this much before.

"Don't you think that us having a conversation is a bad idea?" He wasn't going to fall onto a land mine without an attempt to test the terrain first.

"While I realize talking to me is low on your list of preferred activities, what do you suggest we do for the next hundred and fifty miles of scrub and cacti until we start picking up cell-phone coverage again? Crank the radio and hear one of the sexy songs you wrote about me while I slowly became your untouchable muse instead of your living, breathing girlfriend?"

Romero blinked, trying hard to focus on the road while processing her words. He did *not* want to fight. Would not fight with her. She was clearly spoiling for another go-round but he had no desire to pick through this latest accusation he only half understood.

Untouchable?

He'd never been able to keep his hands off this woman when they were together, except for the weeks when he'd had to bury himself in his work. Writing drained him the way nothing else did, but he hadn't realized she took it so personally until that night she'd let loose after the hiking-boot incident.

But, damn it, aside from those times when he needed to write, their relationship had always been hot. And Shannon had as much enthusiasm for sex as she did for everything else in life, a fact he'd better not dwell on now or he'd never make it back to L.A. without pulling over and reminding her how freaking touchable she was.

"How about a neutral CD with none of my songs?" He flipped open the tray in the dash where he kept his music, needing a diversion fast. "We can compromise with some old Aerosmith or Nirvana…" He dug deeper until he found one of her CDs, and even went so far as to offer, "Or we can play some Gretchen Wilson."

Spearing one manicured hand into the CD tray, she retrieved the jewel case and shoved it into her pink faux-leather satchel. As a diehard vegan, she didn't do real leather.

"You took Gretchen with you when you left? Bad

enough you had to make sexy eyes all through the reception at the fawning groupie who swore she loved you since your days with Jinxed." Shannon clutched her heart like a devoted fan and raised her voice an octave. "*And I saw you in Dallas and Houston and Austin and Shreveport—* Geez. I thought for sure she was going to whip off her double-D bra and fling it your way to make her point."

Romero eased the accelerator down again, deciding eighty miles an hour would be a better option than more hours of this. Any minutes he could shave off this trip would be a good idea.

Besides, there was a VW van behind them that had been riding his bumper for the past five miles. Which was ironic as hell, since there wasn't another vehicle in sight.

"Sexy eyes?" Having grown up in a household full of argumentative types, he took pride in the fact that he didn't rile easily. He was a pro at avoiding conflict. But if she kept this up, he didn't see how he'd keep a lock on his cool.

"Yes." She made an expansive gesture with her hands that was automatic when she got excited. Or mad. "Men's eyes turn all hot and bothered when they're mentally undressing someone."

The van behind them was still bearing down on the sports coupe, so Romero didn't address the fact that there was no such thing as hot and bothered eyes.

"What the hell is this guy doing?" he muttered instead.

Shannon turned in her seat to peer out the back window, her long blond hair brushing his shoulder and pooling on the console where his hand rested on the stick shift.

"Can't you outrun him?" She straightened to look at him, her body close to his the way it had been during that one electric dance they'd shared at the wedding reception.

If anyone made him have sexy eyes, it was this woman. Mentally undressing her was pretty much second nature whenever he couldn't indulge in the real thing.

"What are we, sixteen years old?" He didn't plan to drag race with some crappy vehicle a car owner would be only too glad to total for the sake of an insurance settlement.

The van swerved out into the other lane on the narrow road, and for a moment, Romero thought he would simply pass them.

"He's going around us anyway." Shannon's eyes followed the vehicle as it pulled up beside them.

Romero slowed down to let the guy pass, glad to be getting rid of him. But the jackass in the van veered closer.

"Hey!" Shannon yelled, a moment before the van swerved hard into the driver's side of the Beemer.

The scrape of metal on metal seared through him. Romero yanked the steering wheel hard to the right. His tires squealed and one popped as the rubber raked through rocks alongside the road. Scraggly Joshua trees appeared in front of the windshield and the car went airborne as they sliced nose-first down a steep embankment.

Shannon screamed. His predominant thought as the rocky desert rose up to meet them was that he'd give anything to make sure nothing happened to her. When the nose collided with the gritty ground at the bottom of the slope, bits of plastic and metal mangled and crunched until the impact reached the main frame. The steel encasing them fought back and the car bounced down onto its roof.

Romero reached blindly for Shannon, his brain scrambled and blood somehow in his eye as he turned to look for her. He saw a curtain of long blond hair brushing the ceiling and his heart lodged a little deeper in his throat.

"Shan?" His hand found her shoulder and came back sticky.

She was bleeding. The thin trail of blood seemed to originate at the back of her head.

"Shannon?"

He blinked to try to clear away the red haze in his vision. The scent of smoke and burned rubber stung his nose.

Smoke?

Like a bat out of hell he grabbed for his seat belt to free Shannon before the car caught on fire. He might not have lived up to her expectations as a boyfriend, but he damn well would never let anything happen to her.

2

SHANNON BECAME AWARE of the burning odor slowly.

Her neighbor's cooking was iffy, but she could never remember anything this acrid wafting from next door in the year since she'd bought a house with Romero. A house Romero didn't share anymore. Besides, she couldn't be at home, because her bed was way more comfortable than this. Hard objects speared into her back. Water dripped down onto her face. Her lips.

She ran her tongue along her mouth to catch the droplet, since her throat was dry. Only it wasn't water. It was sweat.

"Shannon."

"Romero." Her whole mood shifted as she got her bearings.

She felt him stretched out over her, his hot male body drenched and hard. She couldn't wait to open her eyes and see it for herself. See him. The man was sex personified.

She reached for him as she wrenched her eyelids open. And, oh, man, Romero Jinks rated high on a woman's list of faces she'd like to see when she woke up.

He leaned over her, his dark eyes narrowed with concern. His angular face was drawn into stark lines, while a cut oozed blood just below his right eyebrow. He was part Irish and part Mexican, a heritage that had blessed him with inky dark lashes and silky black hair. Women around the globe lusted after him, but for this moment at least, Shannon had him all to herself.

Too bad her head was throbbing with pain at the time she'd managed to snag the honor.

"Are you okay?" His hand skimmed up the back of her neck and the grit against his fingertips made her realize she was lying on the dirt.

There'd been an accident.

Her fingers reached for her Celtic necklace, the only item she wore that meant something to her. She could replace the Louboutin shoes—although perhaps not too soon considering her new budget—but the necklace had been her mother's. One of the few pieces of jewelry that hadn't been all about the bling, since cinema sex icon Bridget Leigh had received it long before her life goals involved bringing the men of Hollywood to their knees.

Hollywood had turned out to be a bigger, badder enemy than even her mother could have predicted, driving her to her death before she'd had a chance to overcome her addiction to prescription painkillers. After dealing with a death that had turned into a media frenzy, Shannon had tried to step out of her mother's shadow and be taken seriously as an actress, a dream that never really took off. And a dream that never would if she accepted film roles like the one Ceily had been waving in front of her nose. Another flesh movie about her mother's life.

Shannon hadn't even bothered to read the script.

"I'm fine. How about you? You're bleeding." She inched upward before realizing she was practically clinging to Romero for support. Shannon released him in a hurry—she wouldn't let an adrenaline rush send her back to his arms. Not after he'd addressed her relationship frustrations by suggesting a trial separation. She'd been too devastated by the idea to argue. Besides, the man *didn't* argue. He expected people to either be happy with him or, she'd discovered, to be out of his life completely.

"It's nothing. But you've been unconscious for a few minutes. Are you sure you're all right?" He cradled the back of her head and her nerve endings danced at his nearness.

How many times had he stroked those long, guitar player fingers over her body to elicit soft sighs until he hit just the right note? The temptation to arch up and kiss him, to drag him down to the hard ground with her, was strong.

But hadn't that been the trouble with them all along? They'd always been so willing to lose themselves in sex, ignoring their problems until they were so monumental that the lack of a pair of hiking boots in a woman's size six could detonate an entire relationship.

"I'm fine." She struggled to sit up the rest of the way, needing to escape the touch that had the power to render her brainless in zero to sixty. "But what was with that guy in the van?"

Romero frowned at her, as if he didn't believe for a minute she was fine, but at last his disarming fingers fell away from her scalp, and he dropped back to sit on his butt in the sand.

They were in the middle of nowhere. No houses or buildings, no signs or highways. Far above them Shannon could see the edge of the road they'd been on, but the embankment was so steep it would be hell to try to climb back up there. Besides, now that she thought about it, she hadn't seen any houses or buildings on the route they'd been driving. Apart from the van that had run them off the bumpy back road they'd traveled in the hope of taking a shortcut, she hadn't seen signs of civilization for miles.

"I don't know, but he had a California state license plate, and you'd better believe I'm going to report his ass to the insurance company." Romero drew in his long legs, dropped his elbows onto his knees and speared a hand through his hair. "But I don't have a clue how we're going to get help."

"You tried the cell phones?"

"Not yours, but mine doesn't work and the navigational system in the Beemer is out, so I'd say there's no coverage here."

Shannon patted her pocket for her phone and couldn't find it. "Mine must have fallen out of my jacket when we flipped." She started to stand. "I'll go check—"

"No." He gripped her arm tightly, holding her next to him. "The car smelled like something was burning. You'd better give it time until we're sure nothing could ignite."

Sinking back to the sand beside him, she tried to ignore the feel of his hand on her, the warmth of his palm penetrating her jacket to the skin beneath. The firm hold did something dizzying to her senses. She wasn't some hard-core S and M chick, but she loved to be dominated. It was a fantasy she'd felt safe enough with Romero to share. A fantasy he'd been incredibly skilled at indulging to just the right degree.

Apparently, he'd been sharing some of her thoughts, because his gaze heated for one sizzling second before he released her, turning his attention back to the smoking car.

A wise woman would do the same.

She shoved aside images of Romero pressing her up against their bedroom wall and wrenching her clothes off in a fevered frenzy. Instead, she focused on the BMW perched on its roof, the front end smashed beyond recognition while the radiator hissed steam. A bold blackbird landed on one tire, undeterred by the potential for an explosive situation.

"Thank you for getting me out of there." She couldn't show her gratitude by covering his gorgeous mug with kisses, so she settled for the old-fashioned method. "I don't remember us landing or you pulling me out, but you must have."

Her heart squeezed at the thought of how close they'd come to death. If the car hadn't been so well engineered they might not be sitting here right now.

"I'm glad you're okay." He shot her a sideways look. "Even if I am a self-absorbed bastard with no appreciation for anyone else's feelings."

She recalled the accusation, one of many she'd launched at him during their fight. One of many he'd simply accepted and hadn't argued about. The fact that he didn't care enough to argue, to fight for their relationship and *her,* that had hurt her far more than the lack of hiking boots, or his inconsistent schedule that dragged him away for months on end, then planted him back home for weeks straight, only to hide out in his basement recording studio.

"Yeah, well, clearly you're having a good day." She rose to her feet, unwilling to face more reminders of their breakup. The loss of him was still an open wound for her even though he'd been able to roll right on with life without missing a beat. "If that car hasn't exploded by now, I'm not going to worry about it. I'll see if I have cell coverage so we can get out of here."

Shannon wobbled on her heels in the sandy terrain, her unsteadiness as much from her head injury as her impractical shoes.

"Are you in that much of a hurry to leave me?" he called after her.

"I'm not the one who likes to run away when the going gets tough." She shot the accusation over her shoulder. "But I think you'd agree we'll both be better off when this trip is over and we can go our separate ways."

SHE HADN'T TOLD HIM anything he didn't already know.

Romero was well aware that she'd had enough of him. That had been abundantly clear during the daylong rampage when she called his bluff on the trial separation idea and moved straight ahead to removing him from her life completely. She'd still been spoiling for a fight when he'd pulled out of the driveway with a bag in hand. But he couldn't help a twinge of regret that she still harbored some resentment toward him even now, when they'd nearly died. Would she have shown up in front of St. Peter's gate with her score sheet in hand of all the times Romero had ticked her off?

"You're a hard woman to please," he muttered, and

got up, unwilling to let her be blown up in the hunt for a cell phone that wasn't going to work anyhow.

"I disagree," she replied as she hunkered down near the open window of the Beemer and peered inside. "I'm an easy woman to please for people who are willing to engage in the occasional disagreement to work through problems in a relationship."

Romero's head pounded with frustration about the car, the accident and the long walk he feared was ahead of them, so Shannon's latest slam seemed poorly timed.

He bracketed her hips with his hands and hauled her out of the way so he could find her phone for her. She huffed and puffed about it, but he knew damn well she wouldn't want to crawl around in an upside-down car to retrieve her things.

"Do you have some kind of bionic hearing or what?" He couldn't imagine how she'd heard him talking to himself twenty yards away from her.

"Hardly. My hearing just *seems* good to you by comparison because you don't like to listen and, as a result, hear very little."

He picked her cell off the visor and removed her purse strap from a bar it was caught on under the passenger seat. Handing both items out to her, he then grabbed his wallet out of the glove box along with some tissues and a first-aid kit.

"What are you doing?" she asked as he removed the keys from the ignition and brought them around to the back of the car.

Finally, words from her mouth that were not arrows aimed at him.

"I'm going to get our suitcases out so we can stream-

line what we need." He pried open the trunk with con-
siderable effort, since that had bent, too, but the moment
he released the latch, all the suitcases dropped out to the
ground with a thud.

"What?" Shannon paced in a nervous circle, her
shoes kicking up dirt as she walked, so a dust cloud
formed around her ankles. "I haven't even tried my
phone yet. And we don't know that the car won't work
at all, do we?"

He sent a meaningful look toward the upside-down,
torn-up automobile.

"But if we could flip it—"

"It would still have a blown tire, a bent front axle and
a slew of engine parts that broke during the fall. Trust
me, the vehicle serves no purpose." He took his keys out
of the trunk and didn't bother to shut it.

"Do we even know where we are?" She bit her lip
as she stared down at her phone, and Romero knew she
couldn't get a signal.

"Shannon, there's no phone service." He tugged the cell
away from her and dropped it in her jacket pocket. "Something like twenty percent of Mexico doesn't even have
electricity, so there are definitely large pockets without cell
coverage. We need to figure out which way to walk that
will yield some sign of life first. Any guesses?"

"Walk?" Her fingers crept back up to the chain she
liked to wear, the one with the Celtic knot, and began
to slide the pendant along the links.

It occurred to him that he knew she loved that necklace, but he didn't have a clue why. For all he knew it
could be a bauble from another boyfriend—he'd never
thought to ask. The realization tweaked his conscience

until he reminded himself he'd been on tour for something like a hundred and fifty days in the past year. Was it any wonder they hadn't ever really known each other?

The sun cooked the countryside despite the fact that it was February, the heat reflected back by the pale sand beneath their feet. A lizard darted over his boot and he noticed the profound silence that came with being lost in the middle of nowhere.

"C'mon, Shan." He burrowed in his overnight bag and found a bottle of water to hand to her. "I've seen you rock the treadmill for ninety minutes and knock off almost ten miles. I'm sure you can manage a walk to the next town."

She took the water bottle from him and he noticed two of her nails were broken and the back of her hand was scraped up, no doubt from the accident. He cursed the driver of that van all over again.

Damn it, he would find a way to prosecute that bastard once they returned to the States, no matter what a pain in the butt it was to chase someone down for a crime committed in another country.

"I'm usually a little better equipped for running when I hit the treadmill." She cracked the bottle top and took a sip. The movement of her lips on the container transported him to other times and places, romantic dates when he'd watched her sip vintage champagne from long-stemmed crystal or purse her mouth around a Jell-O shooter when they went out with friends. Something about the way she moved those full lips reduced him to seeing her through a slow-motion lens, and he had to blink his way out of the encroaching sex fog. He'd lost the right to fantasize about her lips when he'd peeled out of their driveway.

Funny about that—*their* driveway. No house he'd ever lived in felt as much like home as when they'd moved in together. The pricey piece of real estate had become a haven in no time. And although the house had been a joint investment, he was in no hurry to sell it or see her move out. He'd been staying in a hotel until he figured out where to go next, but he didn't want to think about living in a house without her in it. Her fashion-conscious dogs. Her frequent ventures into ethnic cooking, from Norwegian to Thai. Her impromptu parties.

"Romero?" She waved a hand in front of his eyes and he remembered how much it drove her crazy when he zoned out.

She figured he wasn't listening, and maybe she was right, since he didn't have a clue what they'd been saying. He'd worked so damn hard to shut out his overbearing family from an early age that he'd carried the habit into all his other relationships, including a failed quickie marriage before Shannon. The complaints of his ex-wife hadn't been all that much different from the frustrations Shannon had expressed.

He just didn't know how to fix it. A damn shame, since losing Shannon had hurt even more than the breakup of the marriage he'd rushed into. He missed the spark she'd brought to his life with her nonstop energy and her insistence that he enter the world now and then. Before he'd met her, he liked to hole up between tours, working on his music in solitude. But he'd discovered a new way to relax with Shannon, a way to hang out with friends and experience a quiet life without going to ground.

"How do you expect me to walk through the Mexican

desert dressed in jeans and three-and-a-half-inch heels?"

Romero peered around at the scrub and patches of grass scattered around the landscape. A thick stand of low trees loomed fifty yards away from where the Beemer had crashed down the embankment.

"Actually, the Sonoran Desert is one of the more kind terrains as far as deserts go because—"

"That's not the point!" She screwed the cap back on the water and thrust it toward him, her silver bracelets jingling with a resonant hum like a cymbal. The dull thump of her foot on the ground broke the melody. "Don't you see that I've got nothing to wear for hiking around Mexico?"

He scowled, acknowledging this was a cause for concern. He'd brought comfortable clothes for traveling, but Shannon didn't ever seem to dress that way. Even her exercise outfits looked like something she could go clubbing in at a moment's notice. Not once in all their time together had he known her to put on a pair of cutoff sweats and a tee for a workout, but then, she'd been hounded by the paparazzi all her life as the daughter of a megastar. She'd confided in him once that she didn't dare have an "off" day or she'd be roasted in the tabloids for weeks afterward, and with the number her mother had done on her, Romero gathered that she didn't deal well with too much public scrutiny.

"I've got a shirt you can wear." He wouldn't have made the offer unless they were in dire straits, since seeing her in his clothes made him seriously hot for her. And possessive as hell.

Then again, looking at a woman in your clothes was

only one step away from seeing her with your rock on her hand, and Romero didn't have any intention of taking that kind of step no matter how possessive he felt about someone. He'd witnessed firsthand how marriage could change a person, with that ill-advised union in his twenties. For that matter, he and Shannon had probably started growing apart the minute he'd made the big leap of faith and asked her to move in with him. He'd try like hell to remember the fact once his Ramones shirt was hugging Shannon's breasts.

She moved closer to him, frowning down at the contents of his overnight bag as he retrieved the worn black cotton.

"I'm not worried about my clothes so much as my shoes. I only brought high heels for the wedding." She tucked his shirt into her bag, as if to put it on at a later date, then dropped down onto a flat rock near his leather satchel and stretched her long legs out in front of her.

The same long legs she used to wrap around his waist. Or twine around his in bed when she wanted him to touch her. He could see the outline of her thighs in the taut fabric of her jeans, long slender muscle neatly defined from all those hours on the treadmill. All that time in his bed.

"I can't help you with the shoes," he admitted, determined to focus on the problem at hand and not give in to another slow-motion inventory of the ways Shannon Leigh was sexy.

"Yeah. I guess you can't help me with the shoes." Her voice went flat. Cold. "Pretty damned ironic that this would have been the perfect time for me to have a pair of freaking *hiking boots.*"

Okay, so he'd walked right into that one. But if she thought he was going to engage in her war of words when they had hours of walking ahead of them, she had another think coming. He wouldn't do the argument thing on a good day. And frankly, today sucked monkey butt.

He just hoped they found civilization faster than he feared they would, because while Shannon might have reached her boiling point with him, she had yet to see his. But, sure enough, it was building.

And the fallout wasn't going to be pretty.

3

UN-FREAKING-REAL.

Big, ugly birds screeched overhead, and Shannon wondered if they were vultures as she pounded out random combinations of numbers on her cell phone. Maybe she could somehow jar the unit into working before the scavengers started to close in. How could she be in the middle of nowhere with a bunch of noisy birds, no real walking shoes and a man who'd put her heart through the wringer? They had no phone, no map, no navigational system, no car. Thankfully, Romero had traveled with two cases of water in the trunk, since he refused to drink any liquid besides alcohol while south of the border.

He unpacked bottle after bottle from the shrink-wrapped carton now, loading up his overnight bag with Evian. His movements were sharp, quick. Angry. His obvious decision to take the higher ground and not engage in an argument with her about the hiking boots might be admirable if he hadn't taken that route every single time she'd ever had a bone to pick with him. How could they ever solve their problems when he refused to acknowledge them, let alone discuss them?

Residual frustration simmered inside her, but what

was the point of rehashing old terrain? He obviously hadn't thought their relationship was worth fighting over three months ago, since he'd lit out of town on two wheels. She'd heard he'd gone to stay with friends out on Catalina for a few weeks, then he'd taken up residence at a posh Beverly Hills hotel. And in case she wanted to know how he was faring, the supermarket newspapers posted pictures of him tooling around town on his motorcycle or attending glitzy music awards shows. She had no reason to think he'd want to defend his decisions or talk through their issues now.

She'd be better off focusing on getting out of Mexico and back to civilization, away from scrubby bushes and carnivorous birds. She would put Romero behind her. And with any luck, she'd make him eat his heart out at his loss, to boot.

Not that it would be easy while trekking through the desert in jeans and a blazer, since she couldn't wear his T-shirt without getting seriously turned on. The scent of him lingered in that cotton, as did memories of other times he'd worn it. Other times she'd taken it off him. Hence the need to stuff the thing directly into her bag. But she would find a way to make him regret that he'd left her. Wasn't that a woman's best revenge? To have her ex realize he'd made a colossal mistake?

Sauntering over to the spot where he worked to strip down the contents of his bag now overflowing with purified water, Shannon figured she'd better follow his example and sort through the stuff she had to bring with her.

"Do you have any idea where we are?" she asked, just because she hated pronounced silences.

Her mom had been either depressed or bored with her life for as long as Shannon could remember, and her silences had always meant trouble was brewing. Usually that she'd overstayed her welcome wherever her mom was filming and that Shannon would be on her way back home with a nanny before long. She'd worked damn hard to keep her mom too entertained to fall into the long silences and then send her away, but she'd had even less success as a daughter than as a serious actress.

"I tried to take a shortcut off Route 1 back in Insurgentes, where the interstate veers east before coming back west. But I stopped seeing signs a good five miles before we were run off the road."

She recalled they hadn't noticed any other vehicle besides the van once they'd left the main route, so even if they could scale the embankment they'd fallen down, it wouldn't do much good to wait for traffic on a road that had looked more geared to ATVs than real cars. "So we can either backtrack to the highway or try to cut northeast and see if we can meet up with it ahead of us."

She unzipped her biggest suitcase, the vintage trunk, one of her favorite pieces of luggage, and wondered how she would leave anything behind. Even though they couldn't see any other signs of two-legged life right now, that didn't mean looters wouldn't crawl out from the bushes to make off with her stuff.

"Right." Romero dug a knife out of a tool kit that had fallen out of his trunk, and stuffed it inside the bag he apparently planned to bring with him. "But if we backtrack, we know the phone won't work for the whole trip. Whereas if we move forward, we at least have the possibility of finding some kind of cell coverage."

Shannon glanced at her bridesmaid dress, her curling iron and her hot rollers. None of them would be helpful on a journey through the Mexican desert, but she couldn't see herself leaving all of it behind either, especially as the dress was the single most expensive item in any of her suitcases. Romero's trunk latch had broken when he forced it open, so they couldn't lock it up again. Tugging out the pink garment, she rolled it up tight to pack in the medium-size carry-on bag.

"You're not bringing that with you." Romero seemed to be cutting the carpet out of the BMW, for no real purpose that she could see.

"Did I tell *you* what to pack?" The sun overhead went behind a cloud and she noticed for the first time the day turning overcast. The ugly birds that had been stalking them had taken off, but she didn't know if that meant impending bad weather or that the carrion-eating rats with wings had gotten tired of waiting for them to die.

"No, but that's because I have the greater good in mind instead of thinking about what to wear tomorrow." The carpet he'd been sawing at flopped on the ground, the underside stiff and rubberized.

"I'm not wearing this dress tomorrow." In fact, she'd never wear it again, since the first thing she had to do when she returned home, after feeding her dogs, was post the garment on eBay to try to make a little money back on the ridiculously expensive piece. "But it's Vera Wang. I can't bloody well leave it in the desert for thieves."

Any woman of Shannon's acquaintance—and most of the men, for that matter—would have understood. A vein in Romero's temple throbbed so hard it looked like it might well explode.

How could he walk out on her without a fight, and yet a dress brought out the ferocious beast in him?

"I think thieves are the least of our problems. Put the dress back and take the rest of the water I couldn't fit in my bag." He exaggerated the articulation. Clearly, he thought she was a moron.

"You know I may not have all the right survival skills to make it in the Mexican desert." It looked like a freaking desert to her, damn it. She tossed bottle after bottle of water on top of the Vera Wang as a compromise. "But I've lived in Hollywood on my own since I was fourteen, becoming an emancipated minor at sixteen after my guardian aunt spent all my mom's fortune." Not that her personal history wasn't known by every Hollywood insider, outsider and tabloid, considering her mother's fame. "That means I've been *surviving* for over a decade in a jaded jungle full of people who wanted to tear me down, or at the very least, expected me to turn into my druggie mom. And not only have I managed to have a successful career—" okay, so she'd fudged that part, but this was *her* rant "—I've also never been photographed naked, never threw up in a night-club, never got in a fight with the paparazzi, and not once did I cave to addictions that spit people out by the dozens every day in Los Angeles. The mere fact of my existence speaks to my intelligence, don't you think?"

When she had all the bottles of water in her bag, she zipped it up and stared at him, daring him to tell her what to do again.

"I hope you've got everything you need in there, since you don't have an ounce of space left." He glared meaningfully at her bulging bag.

She didn't. She had to have her face cleanser and a few other toiletries. But she could stuff those in the side pouches, couldn't she? She was about to fire off a sharp retort when she remembered the movie script. Even though the treatment was for some crummy indie film cashing in on her mother's fame, her ass would be grass if someone else got their hands on the screenplay and leaked it.

"Crap."

Romero was at least wise enough to go back to peeling the carpet out of the trunk instead of gloating. Maybe that was a benefit to being with a man who never argued. He didn't jump down her throat when she messed up, either. Sighing, Shannon sank to her knees to retrieve the one item she couldn't jam into some tiny side flap. The padded manila envelope contained the project that represented Shannon's only offer to stay in Hollywood. Not that she was taking it.

From Ceily's description, Shannon knew the movie was about her poor mother's arrival in Tinseltown, and her rise to fame that had included nude spreads in a variety of men's magazines and rumors that she'd used sex to get some of the industry's juiciest roles. Later, she'd descended into drugs, alcohol and depression. Nothing the public hadn't heard about before.

Baby Doll would be a movie about a woman's use of sex to get her way—a theme Hollywood producers loved. But Shannon had managed to have a sixteen-year career without taking her clothes off or playing the sexpot. Her mother had been famous for both, blazing through Hollywood with studio directors and producers panting at her heels. Bridget Leigh had elevated sensuality to an art form.

No, Shannon didn't want to do a movie focused on all the things she resented most about her mom, the things that took Bridget away from her daughter before they could fix their dysfunctional relationship. But the script couldn't stay here, either. Vera Wang would have to go.

"Is that the proposal for the film about your mom?" Romero had set aside his knife and rolled up the carpet tightly with a bungee cord around it.

He stuffed the long roll into an elastic side strap on his overnight bag, which was more functional than label conscious. Romero had never been about high fashion or glitz, even in his days with bandmates who wore eyeliner like it was going out of style. Hence his decision to invest a few grand in a new brand of hiking boots to help give the fledgling company a PR boost. He liked to fish on the weekends and take a boat out to Catalina.

"Yes." She hadn't wanted anyone to know she was desperate enough even to consider this kind of film. Especially not a man she wanted to eat his heart out. "I'm probably not going to do this project, since I have a lot of other things in the works."

Like a play so far off Broadway she'd probably be playing Staten Island.

"But it's important enough to sacrifice the Vera Whatever for it." He retrieved some energy bars from his glove compartment before moving to where she bent over her suitcase, firing water bottles out onto a thin brown patch of grass.

Thunder rumbled in the distance.

His nearness rattled her far more than the threat of a downpour. They were even closer than they'd been in his car. His knee grazed hers. The veins on his bicep bulged from his battle ripping out the carpet. The scent of clean male sweat mixed with the bay rum of his soap in some kind of alchemy wizardry that created an instant aphrodisiac. Or maybe that was just because thinking about sex was easier than picking through her reasons for saving the script over the monetarily valuable bridesmaid's dress.

"It's not my script to leave in the middle of the desert." She dodged further argument, stuffing the treatment into her suitcase and packing the pink dress back into the larger of her suitcases, which would have to remain with the ruined automobile. "Much as I might like to line a few birdcages with some of the tripe I've read about my mom."

Shannon watched his broad hands wrap around one water bottle after the next as he repacked her smaller bag, her body remembering the feel of those warm fingers stroking up her back in the night. He'd told her once that the length of his fingers made it easier to play guitar. Musician's hands. But she'd been as impressed with the way he played her body, always able to coax a response from her no matter how tired or overwrought she felt from the daily grind of life on the set.

God, she'd almost forgotten how great those days had been. She'd spent so much time alone while he'd been on tour. Then, even after he'd come home, she had lost him to his music all over again while he'd worked on a new CD. Maybe she'd put too much emphasis on talking, since right now she could picture herself being damn content with not speaking at all and just…touching.

"You don't like the film because it's low budget." Romero zipped the bag, his forearm brushing her knee. The contact made her eyes flutter and threaten to close. She loved that sensation.

"Among other things." She forced herself to focus on what he was saying. The film script. "Even the pictures I made that went straight to DVD were at least produced through major studios. Distribution was assured."

And *she'd* been assured her performance would at least be viewed by more than a few hundred people. She didn't need huge financial rewards from her work, but she dreamed of her skills being appreciated. Her talents shared.

Another clap of thunder made her shove the large suitcase beneath the protective shelter of the overturned car. If there was any chance thieves didn't steal her stuff, she'd rather not have it water damaged.

"In the music business, great work is usually produced by people who have more freedom to follow their vision. Maybe that script you're afraid to read will surprise you."

She rocked back to sit on her heels just as the first raindrop kissed her cheek.

"I'm not afraid to read it." *Liar.* That's why it had been shoved in the back of a drawer since she'd received it a few days after Romero walked out. She'd known the project was coming, and had discussed it with him briefly in the days before he left. She was surprised he even remembered, since he hadn't commented much at the time.

He'd been in his quiet, brooding musician phase.

"Whatever." He got to his feet and held a hand to her to help her up. "If you don't want to take a risk on something more artistic, I understand."

Shannon nearly fell right back on her butt. Then the heavens opened up and doused them, saving Romero from seeing the smoke pour from her ears at the insult he'd just sent her way with so little thought. He pointed east, apparently showing her the direction they'd be taking on this hike from hell to get back to civilization.

He understood if she didn't want to make a *more artistic* movie? Like the rest of her pictures had been total dreck? Besides, this would be a skin flick, wouldn't it?

Her feet moved alongside his, her toes already protesting the three-and-a-half-inch heels, which sank into the sand with every single step. He thought she didn't have the creativity to collaborate with a screenwriter? Or did he think she didn't have the acting chops to pull off the kinds of sexually aggressive scenes she would have to play as the notorious Baby Doll Bridget?

She was no damn prude. And she could act, by God, or she wouldn't have been offered some theater opportunities in New York, even if they were a little removed from Broadway's mainstream.

"You think I can't do something artsy? Assuming I'd have the creative freedom to add some depth to this script?" She stopped in her tracks, unable to stew silently the way he could.

Rain ran in rivulets down his face as he turned to look back at her, the drops chasing each other along the stark angles of his chiseled cheekbones.

"It's not that—"

"Then you think it's too sexy for me."

He was silent for a beat too long.

She could hardly believe it, after she'd fought for so

many years to prove she wasn't her mother, and no one in the industry had bought it. Apparently Romero bought it.

"You've always said you didn't want to be remembered for your cup size." He reached for her, smoothing aside a section of hair the rain had plastered to her forehead. "Those are your words, not mine."

Yeah, and they were still totally true. So why was she up in arms about him thinking she couldn't play the kind of role some would believe she'd been born to play? But then, she'd always been the feeler, reacting on instinct, while Romero was the thinker. Maybe he had a point. And she would have some input into a film about her mom? She hadn't even considered that, yet it could be a chance to add some substance to the popular vision of her mother.

But that realization didn't stop her from being just a smidge miffed that he thought she couldn't carry off the role of a screen siren.

"Then maybe I need a little more practice being sexy." A flash of indignation had her stepping out of his reach to peel off her satin blazer. The slick fabric was soaked anyhow. Or maybe she was just looking for a way to make Romero suffer the way she suffered around him.

Shannon let the jacket drop on the ground, where she stood and faced the rainstorm in her lavender-colored tank top. Let him feast his eyes on that for a little while and tell her she wasn't sexy enough.

HE MIGHT HAVE BEEN able to look away if it hadn't been for the rhinestone bra strap.

He'd been semiprepared for the unveiling of those incredible breasts that she'd inherited directly from her bombshell mother. Shannon had one of those bodies that made men go dumb with sex thoughts—it was just an immutable law of nature. She often wore jackets and blazers or the occasional sweater to deflect the inevitable head-turning stares her body brought her way, so Romero had forced himself not to look south of her chin when her little satin jacket came off.

But damned if the glitter of a cheeky bra strap didn't catch his eye. It peeked out from under the cotton tank top now molded to her skin, the shimmering stones wrapping around her shoulder and disappearing under the top just above the start of a bra cup. And, yeah, he could see that, too, since her tank top had turned utterly transparent with the rain.

With an effort he raised his eyes, since he'd never been the type to ogle a woman. He'd been brought up better than that, for one thing. His family may have driven him crazy with the constant bickering, but at least they'd instilled good manners. Plus, he'd been solicited by enough beautiful women over the course of his lifetime that he considered himself fairly immune to something as fleeting as looks. But Shannon had always had a unique effect on him. He'd wanted her for reasons that included sex, yet went above and beyond.

When he met her gaze, her blue eyes flashed with a laser intensity he could only describe as insolent. She'd pushed him and pushed him to fight with her—for the past few hours, three months ago, all freaking year. And now she wanted to taunt him with something he craved very, very much.

Big. Mistake.

He shrugged his bag off his shoulders and stalked

toward her, rainwater pooling around his feet before being absorbed by the sand.

Her eyes widened.

Two more steps brought him toe to toe with her, invading her personal space and making his presence damn well-known.

"Romero?" She bit her lip as she peered up at him. Her breathing came hard, each inhale bringing her breasts into the barest of contact with his chest. A teasing caress that only added to the fire inside him.

A fire she'd damn well started.

"I don't think being sexy is your problem." His hands gravitated to her waist. He knew the layout of her body better than his own, having memorized the spatial relationships of her curves long ago.

He noticed she didn't have one of her smart-mouth comebacks for him now. A good thing, since he had a better idea for putting her mouth to work.

Inhaling the scent of her, which was intensified by the combination of rain and heat, he bent forward, brushing his lips against hers. He speared his hands up the back of her tank top, splaying them over her skin. Her eyelids fell to half-mast and he moved in for the full taste, his mouth as hungry for her as every other part of him.

If she wanted to play sexual instigator, he planned to show her exactly what she did to him.

4

TOUCHING SHANNON TRIPPED a switch inside him.

No, her peeling off her clothes was what had done him in. The challenge in her eyes as they'd stood in the desert downpour had proved even more difficult to resist than her body, and that was saying a lot considering the woman in his arms.

Her flesh felt hot against him, the warmth of her skin coming through her clothes despite the cooling rain streaking over them. She wrapped her arms around his neck, drawing him close while she arched up on her toes. Her hips gravitated to his, his blood running thick and hot through his veins at the feel of her soft curves against him.

He wanted to take her.

The desert fell away along with the rain, the cacti and the totaled car. All that mattered was getting Shannon out of her clothes and all over him, quenching the burning that fired his skin.

He deepened the kiss and lifted her off her feet, needing to touch every part of her within his grasp. She made a hungry sound in her throat, a soft cry that he recognized all too well as her personal litany of desire—a precursor to a sweet chorus of sighs and moans that were better than any music he'd ever written.

"Shannon." Her name fell from his lips between kisses, as if he needed to confirm the fact that the woman coming undone against him was the same one who'd churned up more emotions in him in a year than he'd experienced in a whole lifetime before meeting her.

"You make me crazy," she whispered back, clutching his T-shirt in one hand and a fistful of his hair in the other.

She edged back to look at him while he still held her in the air, suspended off the ground a good couple of inches. His heart slugged hard against his chest, against the softness of her breasts pressed against him, the heat steaming off them where their bodies melded together.

"You make me want to have sex in the middle of the desert." Which was the same as making him crazy, since he'd never do something like that out here in the open during the middle of a flash flood.

He leaned in to kiss her, to take that mouth of hers and have the last word in this argument between them that never ended. At the last second her hand reached up, applying the slightest pressure to his chest.

"I know it's no business of mine now that we broke up. But since you just kissed me, I have to ask—did you sleep with that groupie from the wedding?"

It took him long, drawn-out seconds to process her words, since he was so hot he thought he'd explode. When the meaning finally sank in, the icy chill of reality forced him to set her on her feet.

"What are you talking about?" He shook his head, wondering what had happened to the self-confident, devil-may-care woman he'd fallen in love with. She'd never been the jealous type, leaving him to pursue his interests while she went after hers.

Did she honestly still care who was in his life?

"You danced with her a lot last night." Her eyes were no longer passion-fogged, but clear. Worried. "I saw you walking down to the beach—"

"To get away from all the questions I fielded about you the whole day." He released Shannon completely, his hands twitchy with sexual frustration, especially when he considered how he'd feel if the tables were turned and it had been her dancing with some other guy the night before. Ouch. "And even though you haven't asked, I'm going to tell you—there hasn't been anyone else for me since we split up."

Plucking his bag up off the ground, he turned on his heel and began walking, figuring any direction was a far cry better than being next to a woman who tempted him beyond reason. A woman he hadn't come close to forgetting.

"NO ONE?" Shannon couldn't resist asking for a small point of clarification as she hurried to catch up with Romero, shocked that he had confided something so personal. Something that touched her in spite of everything they'd been through.

"You're a tough act to follow." He didn't even turn to look toward her, his feet trudging to the northeast as the rain pelted him from the right. "And give me credit for having a little more respect for you than to pick up a stranger and take her back to my hotel room when I was staying right across the hall from you. After what we shared."

Shannon didn't know if she felt more relieved that he hadn't been with anyone else or sad that she'd blown an opportunity to get naked with him herself. Probably a mixture of both.

Adjusting the strap of her bag, she followed Romero, her thoughts confused. Her feet sank in the mud as she walked, the skinny heels of her shoes disappearing into the wet sand and somehow becoming vacuum packed into the muck so that the earth made a sucking sound each time she pulled her foot out.

"Well." She didn't have a clue what to say to him, her heart still skipping wildly from his touch even while her brain told her she ought to have a little more restraint where he was concerned. *He* had wanted to separate from *her,* after all. "Thank you for that. I haven't been dating, either, but I know men seem to rebound faster."

Excluding her mom, who had gone through men as fast as she made movies. Maybe that's why Shannon wanted so badly to get her relationships right. She'd seen firsthand how much it hurt her mother to lose each consecutive boyfriend, never realizing how her own actions had played a role in the revolving door in her life.

"I think that's just an illusion." Romero didn't even look back, his long strides eating up the rain-soaked sand. "And I never pictured you as the type to jump into new relationships anyhow."

He'd rolled up the hems of his cargo pants at some point, his clothes staying out of the mud, while her boot-cut jeans dragged along an extra ten pounds of grit as she walked.

He looked as if he'd walked straight off the Discovery Channel, totally unaffected by the conditions. Even the bag on his back with the big swatch of unwieldy carpet fit the mold. She wouldn't have been surprised to see him pull a tent and a canteen out of that pack, but then he liked taking off into the wild sometimes. He hadn't done it much while they'd been together other than some weekend fishing jaunts. But he had the hiking gear, the camping stuff. He'd once told her that his idea of recharging was taking off to the mountains for a couple of weeks.

Without hotel reservations.

"Oh." No doubt that was part of the reason he thought she couldn't do the steamy movie roles. She'd worked hard to keep her image as far from femme fatale as possible. "Can I ask you another question as long as we're finally having a conversation? Why did you bail out in the middle of a fight and never come back?"

She'd actually thought he might return when she'd finally gone to bed that night. She'd been upset with him a couple of times before that, although never to that degree. But he'd always reappeared after the next leg of his tour, or on the set of her next movie, ready to pretend nothing had happened. She'd been devastated the following day when Romero had sent one of the guys from his security team to pick up the stuff she'd packed. Papers from his lawyer had arrived two days later, requesting she keep him informed whether she wanted to purchase his half of the house or set up a time frame to sell.

Her friends had agreed that his disappearing act with the legal follow-up had been kind of harsh, though they'd respected his need to protect a real estate investment. But even though Shannon had nearly bankrupted herself to take over his half of the mortgage payments during the past few months, her unhappiness didn't have a damn thing to do with money. She just didn't understand how Romero could have walked away without a backward glance. A conversation when things had cooled down.

"Did you honestly expect we could go on, business as usual, after the whole neighborhood saw you carrying boxes of my stuff to the curb?" He turned to glare at her, his expression more ominous than the black clouds overhead.

She'd almost caught up to him by the time he finished, but she hesitated to close the distance any more. After months of holding back on her—retreating or otherwise disengaging whenever they fought—he now looked very ready to throttle her.

"And that's what a relationship should be in your eyes? Business as usual? Nothing to cause any disruptions in the smooth surface of your well-oiled record-making machine and rigorous touring schedule?"

Rainwater sluiced over her shoulders and poured down the valley of her cleavage. A chill shook her involuntarily and she folded her arms against the cold. Her heavy carry-on bag cut into her collarbone where she carried it cross-wise to better distribute the weight. Sandy grit coated her feet, rubbing her flesh raw where it lodged between her shoes and skin, her bandage around the broken toenail long gone. Her head still throbbed from where she'd banged it during the accident, although at least she'd had some aspirin in her purse. Romero had cleaned the wound for her, but left it unbandaged because of her hair.

She knew he would prefer she never speak of their breakup again. But was it so wrong to want a little closure after they'd shared so much?

"I think it should damn well support you instead of bringing you down." His gaze swept the length of her body, the heat that had been in his eyes so recently replaced by cool assessment. "Are you going to be able to keep going?"

He hadn't felt supported? She'd compromised more for this man than anyone she'd ever known, save her mother. Shannon had considered his needs—*supported* his needs for silence, for writing time, for alone time, for brooding—continually. At least this reminder of how differently they viewed their time together made their split a little easier to bear.

"You're damn straight I can keep going." Hitching the strap of her bag higher on her shoulder, she stared into those gorgeous dark eyes of his. "Lead the way."

ONLY A JACKASS WOULD keep going.

After two hours of stone-cold silence from the woman behind him while they slogged through the rainy desert, Romero knew with every telling slurp of mud around Shannon's high heels that they needed to stop for the night. They'd wasted a lot of time after the accident getting oriented and coming up with a plan. Of course, he'd also spent a fair amount of time reassuring himself Shannon's head injury wasn't serious. Then things had gotten off to a slow start after their fight about the script and Shannon's abrupt need to prove she was sexy.

The memory of their kiss had made for one damned uncomfortable walk.

And they sure as hell hadn't covered much ground in the unrelenting downpour, which happened only a couple of times a year in the normally dry region. By Romero's calculation, they'd gone five or six miles. It was no wonder they hadn't come across any signs of human life yet. But he hated to admit defeat and stop for the night. His watch assured him it was only five o'clock, but the weather didn't show any sign of clearing before dark.

And Shannon couldn't walk any farther in those shoes. Her feet had to be blistered and sore.

"We're not going to find help today." He halted in his tracks near where a patch of huge, organ pipe cacti rose up out of the Sonoran Desert. "I can barely see four feet in front of me."

"I thought it never rains in the desert," Shannon said, her voice tinged with exhaustion. "Especially this time of year."

She scrubbed a hand along her bare arm and he realized the temperature was dropping. Vaguely, he recalled reading about snowstorms in the mountains at the northern edge of this region—Mexico's answer to the Australian Outback. But they were still far enough south where that wouldn't be a problem. He didn't have a jacket, and even with the rain, he wasn't cold.

"So what do you say?" He hated to make the decision on his own, but Shannon had been quiet for the past couple of miles.

"About what?" She hopped from foot to foot and he suspected she was cold even if he wasn't. "Do you want me to make a guess what our odds are of being found in the middle of the desert at night? Or should I tell you how much I can't wait to camp out in the pouring rain after dark so we can do this all over again t-tomorrow?"

Her teeth chattered and he thought perhaps her lips had turned blue, although colors were tough to detect in the gray light.

Guilt nipped him even though he'd gone over the way he'd been driving and couldn't think of what he might have done differently to have avoided the accident. That driver in the van had seemed locked in the grips of a serious case of road rage.

"I know you don't have the answers." He tossed his pack aside and tugged hers off her shoulder. "I just figured you would have an opinion on what to do next."

She ducked as he pulled her carry-on up and over her head. They'd each had a bottle of water earlier, but that hadn't eased the weight of her bag much. Damn it. Her collarbone had chafed bright red and raw from the strap.

That kind of color he could see well enough.

"I don't have an opinion beyond thinking my poor dogs are going to go hungry tonight and all of our options suck." She shrugged her shoulders and seemed to ease a kink out of her back, the action arching her spine and drawing his attention to all the wrong places. The fact that she could look like a rain-slick video vixen in his eyes despite the layers of grime and her obvious exhaustion only proved what a sex-crazed idiot he was when it came to Shannon.

But as much as he'd rather walk ten more miles in silence to shut out the thwarted attraction of a relationship gone bad, Romero wouldn't do that to her. Whether she would admit it or not, she needed to stop for the night.

"Agreed. And don't worry about the dogs. They know where the bag of food is. Maybe we'll be surprised when we wake up in the morning and the visibility is better. We could find signs of life out there once we can see a few feet past the ends of our noses."

He rolled the sleeves of his shirt and focused on finding some rocks for a fire ring. While they trekked through the desert, he'd picked up anything he thought might burn, and he figured he'd start with that to help Shannon get warm, before he turned his attention to a makeshift shelter. The rug from the Beemer would at least keep the rain off their heads if he could find a way to string it up between some of the big cacti.

"What can I do?" Shannon knelt beside her bag and unzipped a side pouch. "I can't rub sticks together to make a fire or any other Boy Scout job, but I'm sure I could do something."

She pulled her daily contacts out of her eyes and tossed them before she jammed an old pair of tortoise-shell glasses on her nose. She didn't use them all the time, but he happened to know she liked to give her eyes a break from the contacts.

He loved those glasses. They were retro-shaped, the kind of thing a fifties-era starlet would have sported back in the day, sans the rhinestones. And something about the heavy, dark frames only emphasized the softness of everything about Shannon, from her round, Betty Boop cheeks to her full, pouty lips.

Yeah, he'd need this downpour to continue if he wanted to keep a rein on his thoughts.

"You don't need to rub sticks together—I packed the flares from the car's emergency kit. If you grab one from my bag and set it in the middle of these stones, that would be great." He dug two more stones out of the ground from the southern side of a nearby saguaro cactus. "I'll light it once the rain stops."

A lot of the desert succulents grew against that kind of anchor, making it easy for him to find rocks in the dim light. He'd replace them all in the morning before they left, since the Sonoran was home to at least a hundred kinds of plants that couldn't be found anywhere else in the world. If Romero hadn't been torn up about this whole business with Shannon, he might have appreciated the time to see the sights up close. He hadn't taken off for parts unknown in over a year, his life too crazy with the tour and being under contract for new material.

He'd been looking forward to a vacation with Shannon after he finished. A surprise trip to the Maldives. Maybe a trek around India. She had the travel bug as bad as he did, she just hadn't gotten to indulge it over the past year while she'd been trying to salvage her career.

"You keep flares in your car?" Shannon approached his bag, frowning. "You've only had that vehicle for what—less than a month? It's not like you're tooling around in a junker on its last legs."

"Doesn't hurt to be prepared." He'd been on enough broken-down boats, motorcycles and tour buses to appreciate a few tools at hand when the inevitable problems occurred—most often in the middle of the night or in the middle of nowhere.

Usually both.

"It would never occur to me to put something like this in my car." She examined the flares and the handful of other stuff he'd packed near them—the matches, tools, hand warmers and other useful gear that had been in his trunk.

"I know." He strode closer to retrieve the pieces of dried-up cactus, brush and scraps of wood he'd stored in the rolled-up carpet, being careful to keep them covered now as he brought them closer to his fire pit. "That's why I put an emergency kit in that little scrap of a hybrid you drive."

"You did?" She stopped digging through the supplies and stared at him.

He suppressed an eye roll. Typical Shannon. If something didn't have an immediate and direct effect on her life at the moment you mentioned it, the information tended to flow right by her.

"Yeah. You never noticed? You were headed up the coast somewhere for a movie and I was worried about you." He remembered how excited she'd been about that role. She'd wanted him to come to Vancouver for part of the filming, but he'd been in Australia and Indonesia during those two weeks.

The memory made him wish he had that time back—time when they'd been in such a fever to see each other he'd counted off every day until they were under the same roof again. Under the same sheets.

She gave a jerky nod, her hands returning to the flares and matches.

"I remember." Standing, she placed the flare in the middle of the fire ring. "I invited you to Vancouver, but you couldn't be bothered to invite me to Oz."

She handed him the book of matches. And then he saw it in her eyes… Damn. She was serious. She'd expected him to ask her to give up a movie part to be with him.

Yeah, right. He knew how that one would have played out. Then he would have been a selfish bastard for asking her to put his career first. He would have been screwed no matter what he said.

"I don't think you would have wanted to miss out on the movie." He scoped out the terrain to figure out how to construct some kind of shelter. He hadn't exactly packed his car trunk for a survival weekend.

"You never know," she retorted. "I might have surprised you sometimes."

Leaning to one side, she unbuckled her shoe and kicked it off while he tried to figure out what in the hell he'd said. No way would she have passed on a film just to hang out with him on the other side of the globe.

Would she?

"What is that supposed to mean?" He stood back while the heat from the flare caught the brush and wafted steam toward him.

"It means that, in spite of your reputation as Mr. Sensitive Songwriter, you don't always understand so well what other people are feeling." She tossed off her other shoe and then reached for the button on her jeans.

Hell, he'd thought he needed to start a fire to warm her up? It was Shannon who was going to flash-fry him.

"What are you doing?" He couldn't help it if his voice hit an octave he normally only reached onstage.

Panic did that to a man.

"Undressing." She gave him a cryptic grin and shimmied out of her pants, her hips rolling just enough to work the wet denim down her thighs until they slid past her knees and gave him an eyeful of pink satin bikini panties trimmed with magenta-colored lace. "No doubt that surprises you, too, but I plan on rinsing off six pounds of desert sand before I settle in for the night. I'll never sleep with this much grit covering me, and there's enough rain coming down for a decent shower if I'm patient."

He couldn't even access the high-pitched voice he'd had a minute ago; his mouth worked but no sound came out. He snapped his trap shut before she noticed.

"Unless—" Her hand caught in the hem of her tank top and his heart cranked out a bass line that could have rocked a football stadium. "Did you want me to help you with the shelter?"

His eyes glued themselves to the patch of skin above her panties where her hand toyed with the shirt hem.

Damn. Her.

How could she play games like this when their split had nearly killed him?

"No, thanks." His throat scratched out the words while he willed her far, far away from him so he couldn't see even a hint of her. Shannon undressed had the power to turn him stupid.

"Then I'll just take my pilfered hotel soap and find someplace private to put the rainfall to work." She waved a tiny white bar she must have picked up at the resort in La Paz. "And thank you for the emergency kit in my car. I'm sorry I didn't notice something nice that you did for me."

Romero took a hell of a long time processing her words, his brain slowing in direct relation to the amount of skin Shannon flashed in the firelight. Why was she talking about something that had happened months ago?

"No problem. And, Shannon?"

She turned, her wet hair sliding against her shoulder as she looked at him expectantly.

"No more surprises." He glared at her to show her how much he meant it, but her sole response was a smile before she and her pink satin panties disappeared into the darkness.

5

FROSTBITE COULD BE kicking in any minute now, but Shannon figured the risk was worth it to see the look on Romero's face when she'd walked away. She'd wanted him to eat his heart out over what he'd given up, and she suspected he was looking for a knife and fork this very minute.

Petty of her, yes. But, damn it, he'd left her without one single, flipping word. As if he couldn't be bothered to comment on a relationship he'd invested almost a whole year in.

She danced from foot to foot in the gritty sand, trying to keep blood flowing to her extremities despite a drop in the temperature. It was probably still in the high fifties, so frostbite wasn't really a concern. She was just glad to wash off the sand, a task she'd barely finished when the rain finally slowed to a stop.

"Brrrr." She brushed off the excess water as she ran to a nearby cactus and retrieved the plastic bag that she'd wrapped Romero's T-shirt in to keep it dry. She dropped the shirt over her head, inhaling his scent.

In the distance, she could see Romero struggling with the fire. The hissing flames were easy to spot in a landscape with no competing light, no signs of civilization anywhere. As Shannon gathered up her soap and underwear, she watched Romero positioning bits of cacti and twigs from afar, his lean, muscular body burnished bronze by the firelight.

The promise of warmth lured her as much as the man, the thought of him heating her faster than any flame ever could. She knew she'd been unfair to strip off her pants in front of him, but maybe she'd still been stung to think he didn't see her playing a sexy role. He thought she was too conservative. Unwilling to take chances or embrace her sexuality just because she didn't flash the paparazzi while pantyless.

Ha!

How would he know, when he'd never spent any time with her? Sure, she appreciated the comfort of character roles that didn't call for taking off her clothes. That didn't mean she didn't take chances now and then. Or that her roles on-screen were a reflection of who she was in private.

For Romero.

A coyote howled in the distance and she urged her feet to move faster, unwilling to find out if hungry desert predators would like the taste of a California girl for supper. Her bare soles protested the effort, for she'd left her shoes by the fire pit. And even though the heels had given her insane blisters the size of Rhode Island, at least they'd protected her feet from cactus prickles or desert plants with the texture of rusted steel wool.

"There you are." Romero caught her before she ran into him, her head down to better scout out those patches of Brillo Pad on the ground.

His hands felt strange and familiar on her at the same

time. As she peered up at him in the darkness, the struggling firelight outlining him in shadow, she was struck again by the sensation that she hardly knew this man who wasn't afraid to take on the Sonoran Desert in the middle of winter with nothing but a Swiss Army knife and some torn upholstery. She'd never seen that survivor-dude side in the year they'd lived together despite the pup tent in the basement and the snowshoes buried under her beach chairs in the garage.

"What is it?" She wondered why he held her there and why he'd come looking for her in the first place. "Were you thinking about joining me in the shower?"

So sue her for flirting. When he touched her, she couldn't think of anything beyond getting closer to him.

He released her instantly, leaving the warmth of his strong hands just a memory.

"I heard the coyote and didn't know if…" He shrugged. "I thought you might be worried."

He spun on his heel and retreated toward the fire. Away from her. Now *this* man she knew. This was the guy who'd busted her heart open wide by showing her tantalizing glimpses of happiness before bolting. How did he do that?

Frustrated in more ways than one, she followed him, grateful when the fire threw enough light to avoid the brush that might cut her toes. Once she stood by the ring of flames, safely away from the toe torture, she looked up to find Romero wrestling with a ball of twine and a saguaro cactus.

Well, not wrestling, exactly.

More like moving very carefully around a dangerous adversary as he wound a length of twine about the stout desert plant.

"What are you doing?" She stepped closer to him in spite of herself, in spite of the way he'd brushed her off moments ago.

The twine he tied off was attached to half of the upholstery he'd cut out of the BMW, and as she studied his handiwork more closely, she realized he had fashioned a pretty good lean-to out of the carpet. With carpet on the ground and carpet stretched out between a handful of bushes and cacti, Romero had formed a narrow roof and a strip of floor. With the rubberized side away from them and the new carpet facing them, he'd made something fairly rainproof, too. A nice bonus in case the wet weather returned.

"I'm trying to make a spot for you to hide out from the coyotes." He turned to flash a wicked grin her way, his mood none the worse for walking away from her before. "It's not the Beverly Wilshire, but it ought to cut the wind and keep us dry if the rain kicks up again."

He sawed off the end of the twine with his knife and then tucked the tool back in his pocket.

Shannon stared at him—no, technically, she gaped. He'd gone and done something sweet and smart and entirely practical to take care of her. Just like with his insertion of a car emergency kit into her vehicle, he'd helped her without making a production of it. He didn't pander for thanks or praise, he simply took care of business so quietly that she might not notice if she wasn't looking for it.

Or if she wasn't stuck in the desert with him where there was nothing else to do besides notice what the man did.

"As tents made out of car upholstery go, this is really

great," she said finally, wishing she'd been able to understand him better when they were together. Would she have been so frustrated with his long periods of alone time, with his silences, if she'd seen more of what lurked beneath the surface?

Then again, what did it matter if her heart thawed at his quiet anticipation of her needs, when he'd made it clear he was through with her? Nothing changed the fact that he'd left and hadn't come back. That he'd suggested they split in the first place.

"Yeah, well, it beats sleeping in an upside-down car." He stood close to her, no doubt an accident of positioning that happened purely because they were both looking at the lean-to. The warmth of his body heated hers.

At least in the car there was a front seat and a backseat. Which meant there would have been something between them to act as a barrier. What kind of barrier would there be between them in the carpet tent he'd rigged up?

Nada. Zilch. Zippo.

She could already see herself wrapping around him as he slept. Because while her head understood there was no going back to what they had, her body hadn't received the memo.

"I call the side facing west." She stepped back from the shelter, needing to distance herself from him and the heated direction of her thoughts now that she didn't have the rain to cool her down.

"You don't know which way is west." Frowning, he swiped a drop of water from his forehead and left a sand smudge behind.

"But *you* know, so you can make sure I'm facing away from that first blast of dawn over the horizon tomorrow morning." She edged closer to the fire, away from the temptation to smooth away the streak of grit on his skin.

"Yeah? I can do that, but I have the feeling you'll be more than ready to leave the carpet tent behind by sunrise." His eyes wandered over her at a lazy pace before connecting with her gaze again. "Have you ever spent the night under the stars?"

Her skin tingled beneath her clothes as if he'd touched all those places his eyes had been. She grew very aware of her nakedness under his T-shirt, and she peered into the fire to escape the sudden intimacy.

"A couple of times, but those experiences bore little resemblance to this." She packed her soap into her bag, then laid her soaking clothes on some of the sturdier-looking cactus plants.

"Did your mom take you?" His voice softened a fraction and she regretted he had the impression her mother was such a sore subject for her.

Well, she was and she wasn't. She'd gotten over some of her old anger at her mom—for checking out on Shannon early, for not saying goodbye. But that hadn't made the hurt go away. So, yes, her mother was a sore subject. But not necessarily an unwelcome one. Shannon didn't want to forget the good times mixed in with the crazy, out-of-control ones.

"She took a big entourage on a caravan trip in Egypt when I was twelve. Sort of her chance to play harem girl to her desert-prince boyfriend at the time." Mostly, Shannon remembered despising her camel, and the feeling had apparently been mutual. To this day, that humped beast remained the only living creature who'd ever spat at her.

"Sounds like an appropriate trip for a preteen daughter." His movement beside her caught her eye, and she turned just in time to see him tugging his shirt off. "I don't imagine you were sleeping in Coleman's best when you were with your mom."

She forced her eyes from his naked pecs and cut abs, muscles he must get from hotel gyms around the globe, since she'd never witnessed a workout in the house they'd shared. The feel of his powerful body so close had her pulling in a steadying breath.

Too bad that maneuver only served to refresh her memory on the scent of his skin. A scent locked in the T-shirt she wore.

"Definitely not." There'd been a time when she'd thought her mom must be royalty for the way she lived. For the longest time Shannon had tried to tell herself she was fortunate to play princess the few times of year she was summoned to wherever her mother happened to be in the world. But eventually she'd seen Bridget's neglect for what it was—an indifference that grew along with her addiction. "She had her own tent city resurrected every night, and every member of the camp had their own silken retreat complete with torches, rugs and fat chaise longues."

That trip had been one of the last times she'd traveled with her, the decadence so over-the-top even a kid had enough social conscience to recognize the wastefulness. The ploy for media attention.

The total waste of a beautiful talent.

"Are you warm enough?" Romero tossed his wet shirt over one of the taut lines of twine holding up the roof of the carpet shelter, sending water droplets sizzling as they landed in the fire.

Shannon realized her eyes had fastened on him again, her gaze drawn to him in spite of herself. Her heart hammered in her chest and she stood ten feet away from him. What would it be like when she lay beside him with only a few inches of space to separate them? Her breasts ached, and even though she'd warmed up near the fire, the peaks tightened under the thin material of his shirt until she had to wrap her arms around herself to hide her response.

It was going to be a long night.

Romero waited for an answer to his question, but Shannon seemed lost in thought for a long moment. He wondered if she was remembering how her mother had written her off, allowing boyfriends, maids and nannies to raise Shannon. Still, Shannon seemed to have come to a kind of peace about it. Something he admired about her, since he hadn't managed to do the same with his own family, and he didn't have nearly as much reason to complain about his upbringing as Shannon did. He just didn't have the same sensibilities as the rest of his kin.

"I'm warming up." She hugged her arms around herself, his T-shirt doing little to disguise her killer curves. She shifted from foot to foot as if she was uncomfortable.

He watched her breath huff into the cool night air, the puffs of white dissipating as the wind kicked up.

"Are you sure?"

"Mmm-hmm." She nodded despite the chill bumps

on her arms that said otherwise. "Mostly, it's my feet that hurt."

His gaze traveled down to her bare legs and sandy feet. Her bleeding, sandy feet.

"Damn it." He reached for his bag and dragged it closer to the fire. "You shouldn't have worn those shoes."

"They were the lowest heels I had."

He pulled out the wool blanket he'd always kept in his cars, and laid it on the sand.

"Sit." He pointed to the blanket and tunneled around for the bandages and alcohol. "You should have snapped the heels off."

He'd never understood the Hollywood aesthetic that put women—literally—on pedestals.

"They broke after a while anyhow," she muttered glumly as she lowered herself to the blanket, careful to keep his T-shirt tucked around the creamy skin of her thighs. "Is this another Boy Scout must-have? You carry a blanket in the car?"

"Boy Scout?" He pulled her feet into his lap and wiped off some of the grit. "You must not have read my press. They would say I pack a blanket in the car for spur-of-the-moment orgies on the road."

It was an old game they played—trying to outdo each other with outrageous tabloid tidbits. Shannon usually won, since she'd been rumored to be an alien baby back when her mother was pregnant with her. Romero might have had a long career, but considering Shannon had been a subject for media interest even in the womb, her press history had him beat.

"Hmm. You think you're still game for multiple women at once, Hot Stuff? You're not getting any younger."

"You think I'm getting too old for orgies?" When he got the sand cleaned off he cracked open the alcohol. "This is going to sting."

"A sting is preferable to flesh-eating disease. By all means, pour away." She waved him on. "And, no, I don't think you're too old for a few tantric sex tricks now and then. Your number one fan who salivated after you all yesterday at the wedding would have gladly invited four of her best friends to help her get you naked if she thought you might be willing."

Shannon flinched and he halted the flow of liquid over her cuts.

"You okay?"

Nodding, she clenched her fingers around her knee-caps, the gesture bunching up the fabric of her shirt. The cloth shifted all of half an inch. Enough for a man with an eye for Shannon to notice.

"How come you never invited four of *your* best friends to swing with us?" Not that he'd ever ogled any of Shannon's friends, but it never hurt to turn the tables on her.

Something he used to enjoy doing back when they'd found time to talk instead of argue.

"I never needed any help handling you," she retorted, flexing her fingers while the alcohol did its work and Romero glanced over the cut at the back of her head. "But if you'd really wanted to have me crawling all over you with multiple other women, I would have just asked that you reciprocate in kind."

"What?" Good thing he was already sitting down or that bit of news might have knocked him on his ass. "You'd go in for other chicks?"

She'd been a pistol in bed, but he never would have guessed—

A hoot of laughter stopped that thought before it got off the ground.

"No. I'm saying that if you wanted a bunch of girls to satisfy you, you'd have to let me invite a roomful of studs over to gratify me."

His fantasizing ground to a halt.

"That's not funny."

Perversely, she only laughed more.

"It is from where I'm sitting. What is it about men that—"

"Seriously. I don't want to think about you with some other guy." The idea of another man touching her sent his every possessive instinct on red alert.

And, damn it, he'd never been the jealous kind.

Her grin fled and a new light seemed to fire her eyes.

"I was joking. But don't you think we'll both need to get used to the idea of dating other people?" She tugged the shirt down more firmly over her legs and folded her wounded feet underneath her. "When you flee the scene of a relationship, you're basically saying your ex should see other people."

Shannon turned and moved to the far side of the blanket. Away from him.

It was as close as she could get to stomping off into the sunset when they were stranded in the middle of a Mexican desert.

6

SHANNON WASN'T SURE what time it was, since the battery had died on her cell phone, but she guessed about an hour passed before she gave in and turned around from her position on the other side of the fire.

Romero had left her half of a granola bar on the blanket, but he hadn't said jack shit to her after she'd moved away from him. She'd heard him get up and head toward the lean-to about half an hour ago, but she'd been surprisingly absorbed in what she was doing. With nothing else to keep her occupied, she'd pulled out the script for *Baby Doll*, the movie about her mother.

She'd figured she might as well get it over with so she could at least say she'd read it before she passed on it. But the story had gripped her so much that even when the small fire started to die, she'd risked the eyestrain and the cold to read a few more pages.

The script didn't have her mother right. There was a hollowness to Bridget's character. An emptiness that—in the screenplay—she repeatedly tried to fill with sex and fame. But Shannon had observed her mother close-up for fourteen years and read her diaries after her death. She knew that depiction wasn't the whole truth.

The journals were part of a fat envelope given to

Shannon on her sixteenth birthday, after she'd legally won her independence from her money-grubbing aunt. Inside the packet, she'd discovered her mother's private letters, the diaries and the Celtic knot necklace. The envelope had been a window to her mother's heart—a way to know the woman who had been a much-maligned mystery in a lot of ways. Those documents had revealed to Shannon that Bridget hadn't been simply a flawed person trying to fill a void. She'd been learning how to choose her sex partners and her life path after a traumatic childhood stunted by sexual abuse. Ever since then, Shannon hadn't viewed her mother as hardened and brittle, impervious to whomever she hurt on the way up the ladder to stardom. Instead, she saw a hurt in her mother's heart that had never been erased, a hurt she'd tried to ease by indulging in every new experience life tossed her way, even when that involved poor choices.

But in trying to patch up her self-worth with new sensations, and molding herself into the ideal woman in every man's eye, her mom had overlooked the importance of finding love. Or maybe she'd thought she wasn't worthy of it.

Not that Shannon was one to talk. She was thirty years old and hadn't managed any great professional achievement *or* true love.

"Is the movie any good?" Romero called from the shelter of the tent he'd made, his voice scratchy with sleep.

She'd always been amazed the man could fall into the arms of Morpheus while sitting on a tour bus filled with partying band members, but he couldn't think of trying to write a song if she had the TV on or had a few friends over to run some lines for her latest project.

"It's not as bad as I thought it might be." She didn't know how much to confide in him. Then again, maybe she only hesitated to admit she liked it because she knew her reaction merited an "I told you so."

He made his way through the dark toward her, but she couldn't see him until he lowered himself to the blanket beside her. Night loomed thick around them, and having him there next to her made her acutely aware of how cold she'd grown in the past hour as the fire died down. She tucked her fingers under her folded knees to try to warm them.

"Yeah?" He stretched his legs out in front of him, his thigh brushing her hip. "That speaks damn well of the thing, since I know how much you wanted to hate it."

"I didn't *want* to hate it." She fought the temptation to lean into his warmth, her body sending her all kinds of reminders about what it was like to touch him. "I've just seen my mother's memory sensationalized in so many ways that I couldn't imagine some newbie screen-writer would craft any kind of accurate portrayal of her."

"But this is close?" His gaze shifted from her to the script and back again.

She shook her head, and found her hair was still damp from the rain even though the skies had cleared up right after her shower.

"Not really. But the writer chose a lot of interesting moments from her life to show development. It's not just a series of Bridget Leigh on one director's couch after another."

"Don't you think a lot of how your mom is portrayed would come down to the actress who plays her?"

"Maybe," Shannon hedged, wondering why Romero cared anymore what roles she took. "But without a good script to work from, no one is going to know the nuances of the character to play her well."

"Possibly that's why the screenwriter wants you for the part. *You* know the nuances." His throaty voice was magical even in speech. In song, he could melt the heart of girls from eight to eighty years old.

Shannon felt a little melty herself in spite of the cold.

"Too bad I'm not enough of a sexpot to play my mom." She couldn't help remembering his shocked expression earlier when she'd whipped off her blazer to hike around in the rain in her tank top.

Clearly, she hadn't let her inner vixen out to play often enough, no matter that their sex life had been awesome from her perspective.

"I never said that." He shook his head. "You can get worked up faster than any woman I've ever met, you know that?"

A retort about the millions of women in his life teetered on her lips, but she bit it back. Possibly he had a point about a hair trigger when it came to him. But then, maybe she'd used up all her relationship patience early on in life. Her mother's fickle affections had come with a price.

"But let's be honest," she challenged. "You don't see me as having the blatant sexual magnetism my mom had, and I don't blame you, because that's not a card I've opted to play to make it in this business. That doesn't mean I can't scavenge it up when the need arises."

She felt like channeling her inner siren right now, in fact.

"Like for the sake of the right role?" His dark gaze settled on her, unmoving. And in spite of what they'd been through she felt the temptation to fall into that sexy stare and lose herself in his touch.

"Maybe." Or for the sake of seducing the right man. "I'm just not convinced that *Baby Doll* is it."

She still had enough of a career to win a slot in a decent theater production. She wouldn't sacrifice that by selling out for a movie role.

"Maybe you should finish the script first." He reached over her to pull a corner of the wool blanket across her lap, covering her legs.

Her pulse thrummed from that nearness and she fought for some response besides arching her back and falling into him.

"You know as well as I do that no matter how intelligently I portray my mother, I'd still have to engage in some steamy antics on-screen." Steamy antics that right now sounded very appealing. "With the wrong editing, I could end up in a glorified T & A fest while all my best work goes on the cutting-room floor."

Shannon propelled herself off the blanket, wanting out of this conversation and away from the spell Romero could cast on her. But as she limped away from him on sore feet, she realized there was only so far to run. Her options were a fireside chat beside him or the tiny lean-to shelter he'd built to keep them out of the elements for the night.

With a too-hot-for-his-own-good man dogging her battered heels, she was damned either way.

HE COULDN'T WIN.

If Romero went to her now, she'd think he was putting the moves on her. And hadn't she already crushed that notion when she'd reminded him she would soon be seeing other men?

His gut still burned from that wake-up call.

But if he left Shannon to go to sleep on her own, she'd freeze in there. He'd tried sitting close enough to her to share warmth by the fire, but he hadn't pressed the issue while the flames were still sending out some heat. The temperature hadn't hit the freezing point, but it hovered in the high forties, cool enough to make sleeping tough without huddling together.

Damn it.

Getting to his feet, he gathered the blanket they'd been sitting on and shook off the sand. The rainwater had soaked into the ground so fast that none remained to turn the desert floor to mud.

He followed her toward the shelter with heavy steps, wondering how they would survive the night in such close quarters. They'd never had any restraint when they were together before. Why would tonight be any different?

It wasn't just her obvious sex appeal that drew him. He admired the way she'd trekked through the desert with him without complaint, her torn-up feet attesting to how much the hike had hurt her.

He'd seen hints of her steely toughness way back when she'd first mesmerized him on-screen as a love-struck groupie determined to make herself noticed by her idol. Her portrayal had gone beyond the superficial version of an ardent fan to an insightful interpretation of a complicated woman who inspired her idol even more than she was inspired by him. Maybe Romero had fallen for that character a little bit. But in the year that he'd spent with Shannon, he'd noticed she kept a lid on herself between films, and sometimes even on-screen. Part of that, he knew, stemmed from her fears of being compared to her temperamental and passionate mother.

But he missed seeing her uncensored side, something she usually only let show when they traveled someplace the cameras didn't follow. In those first few months when they'd been on the road a lot, she had sounded off more freely with him, sharing her thoughts on everything under the sun while they solved the world's problems over coffee and croissants. He'd loved traveling with her and seeing the world through her eyes, being with her when she didn't have to guard her reputation or be careful not to give the paparazzi any juicy photo ops.

He hadn't fully understood until today how much he'd missed the woman who grabbed life with both hands.

"Shan?" he called to her, giving her fair warning.

The lean-to wasn't much, but at least he'd made enough of a framework to cut the wind. Inside the low opening he'd left for a door, he could see the shadow of movement, but he didn't want to surprise her if she was changing.

Ah, hell, who was he kidding? He didn't dare surprise himself with even the slightest glimpse of Shannon naked or he'd lose whatever control he possessed.

"Hmm?" The sound was too close to the noises she emitted when they made love for his peace of mind.

"I'm sleeping with you." He didn't plan on arguing

the point, and thankfully, she didn't offer up any objections.

Of course, she didn't exactly welcome him with open arms, either. As he ducked inside, she pressed herself back in an effort to avoid unnecessary contact.

Maybe she was as eager to avoid temptation as he was.

"It's been a long time since that happened," she observed lightly as he lay down beside her, twisting his body to avoid knocking into any of the walls.

"Three months." He'd thought of her often enough since then. Getting through the holidays had been hell, especially since he'd found himself checking out a few rings in jewelry-store windows, wondering if he should have taken that insane chance with her....

"Longer than that."

"What's that supposed to mean?" His gray matter was too cold to pick through her words, although his body temp started rising the moment his knee grazed her thigh.

His Ramones T-shirt was sexier than imported silk when the woman who wore it could turn you inside out with a look.

"It means we've rarely shared a bed to actually *sleep*." Her words were surprisingly close to his left ear, her whole body a mere inch away. "So this will be new for us to lie down together and...not touch."

A reminder he could have damn well done without.

His mind traveled back to his first night with her— a date that had turned into seventy-two hours together. He'd been so surprised when she appeared backstage at his show one night, after he'd called her manager a half-dozen times to try to meet her. He'd pursued her because of that groupie movie, because of how she'd captured his imagination on-screen. He'd left messages with mutual friends. Hounded her agent. Sent her tickets to shows when he performed in L.A.

And finally she'd shown up, wearing jeans and a T-shirt with his image on the front, blending in with the crowd and...not. There was some light inside her that set her apart from everyone else no matter where she went. No matter if she was wearing a concert T-shirt or a designer gown. Off-screen, she'd been even more charismatic than on.

"Don't you think it's strange we've hardly ever slept together?" she whispered, her voice pillow-talk soft. Confidential.

He'd never been the type to share a lot of heartfelt intimacies with anyone, but Shannon's curious mind and teasing conversation had a way of drawing him out. Making him want to offer up more of himself to her. Now, in the dark desert night, was no different.

"We didn't really spend that many whole nights together, between the weeks you were on location for a film and the times I was on tour." Those were valid reasons, right? He wasn't going to let her tear down the memory of what they'd shared by nitpicking every aspect that hadn't been textbook perfect.

He'd really thought it could work with her, right up until the end, when he'd discovered she'd been frustrated about far more than he'd realized.

"Plus we never went to bed at the same time." She shifted beside him, the movement stirring the scent of her soap. "And you like to fall asleep in your studio."

Guilt nipped him harder than when Shannon had

read him the riot act all those weeks ago. It had been easy to discount her gripes about him when she'd been whipping his boots across the kitchen. But as they lay side by side in the dark and she pointed out something so basic as never sleeping together, he could see why she'd been disappointed in their relationship.

Maybe he'd just been resisting the kind of traditional setup he'd seen as a child, having grown up in the Midwest in a noisy family full of kids. Romero had been expected to find a wife and start producing offspring like the rest of his siblings. In fact, he still had a "real" job waiting for him back at his father's auto-parts store when he was ready to hang up his guitar.

None of his siblings understood that he couldn't handle that kind of lifestyle. His sisters had quit dishing out *subtle* hints about coming home and settling down a long time ago. By now, the holidays were full-on marriage missions for the Jinks women, so Romero avoided the big family brouhahas wherever possible, in order to dodge the inevitable arguments.

His brief try at marriage to a hard-partying exotic dancer a decade ago had started in a Vegas drive-through chapel and ended six months later—a miserable failure of an experiment that had proved how marriage could turn the most exciting relationship into a monotony of expectations and restrictions on his freedom. He'd never expected to take that risk again, until life with Shannon made him think it could work with the right woman.

"I think that even if we were used to sleeping together we'd have a hell of a time getting any rest on a patch of carpet thrown on a sand pile in this kind of weather." He didn't try to defend himself, knowing she had every right to resent the way they'd lived such separate lives while sharing an address.

Maybe what had been the secret to a successful relationship for him had been the kiss of death for her.

"G-good point." Her teeth chattered.

"Come here." He reached an arm around her, his protective instincts stronger than the need to preserve his sanity, especially now that they were at least communicating in a noncombative way.

"This is a really bad idea," she whispered, even as she laid her head on his chest. Her warm breath puffed softly across his shirt, heating the area above his heart, if only for a moment.

"Afraid you can't resist me?" He bent his head so that his jaw was resting on her silky hair.

And, oh, man, he couldn't even begin to take an inventory of how the rest of her felt pressed against him. His body responded instantly.

"I think you're way too comfortable with being irresistible to women." She splayed one hand across his chest and brushed the smallest caress down the placket of his shirt. She had to feel the answering beat of his heart.

"Is that an admission?" Covering the back of her hand with his, he slipped one finger underneath her palm to trace a circle on the skin.

Her hand trembled and he wanted to think it was because of his touch and not just the temperature outside.

"In light of our estrangement, I plead the Fifth." She reclaimed her hand and inserted it just inside the hem of his T-shirt at his waist.

Her cold fingers wrapped around his flank, perhaps

seeking warmth in a place that she thought wouldn't make him want to grab for her. An impossible task. He couldn't help but flex his other arm.

The one wrapped around Shannon.

All at once he palmed her bottom, squeezing her through the thin T-shirt and pressing her pelvis to his hip. Her breasts strained against his chest and Romero could feel the tight points of the tips.

"Then why don't you let me be the first to admit the truth." Heat roared through him. His blood surged with the need to answer her arousal, to fan the flames so high she'd melt all over him. "I can't keep my hands off you."

7

SHANNON HAD NEVER BEEN able to resist him when he put effort into making her feel special.

If he hadn't checked out on her for long periods of time when they were together, she would still be by his side, her knees going weak whenever he turned his gaze on her. Whenever he touched her.

Like now.

"I'm having a difficult time keeping my hands off you, too," she confessed, her whole body singing with need.

If he moved his hands down a few inches, he'd be touching the bare skin of her thigh. She licked her lips as her mouth went dry.

"Then why are we trying so hard to ignore what we both want?" He lifted a finger to her chin, his face visible beside hers thanks to the moon and stars that filled the desert with a pale glow even at midnight, now that the clouds were gone.

"We don't want to get hurt." She answered automatically and then needed to revise her response. "At least, *I* don't want to get hurt."

She couldn't afford to offer up any more of herself to this man and have him stride away. She'd worked her whole life to build up a reserve of confidence after her mother had shredded hers time and time again. Bridget had ordered her nanny to put her on a diet plan when Shannon had been in the fourth grade. In the seventh, she had suggested Shannon see her plastic surgeon for a nose job. Rewards were doled out if Shannon landed in the gossip magazines, but only if her wardrobe met with Mom's approval.

Shannon had her head on straight now. But she wasn't made of stone. Her heart still had too many vulnerable places and they'd been pricked repeatedly by her flailing career. And by a man who'd made it clear he didn't want another wife, or even a girlfriend who demanded more than an occasional rendezvous in a hotel between takes on her latest film set.

"I didn't mean to hurt you." He reached beneath her chin to tip her jaw up. "You've been good to me in so many ways and you deserved better than me walking out."

Well, color her stunned. It was the first time he'd taken any responsibility for the dissolution of their relationship. She noticed he didn't go so far as to say he regretted leaving her. But the overture touched her anyway.

"You warned me all along you wouldn't make a good boyfriend." Smiling at the memory, she recalled all the times he'd warned her not to get involved with him, even as he flew her to Paris for his night off between shows, or booked tickets to the Aussie coast for a surfing weekend. "After your rants about the way marriage robbed a relationship of its spark and spirit, I knew the odds of us making it were slim."

She knew it logically. But her heart had been ridiculously optimistic she could make it work. He'd married a woman who had been wildly wrong for him, from the sounds of the relationship in old tabloid stories.

Shannon had loved the whole idea of Romero Jinks as much as she loved the man himself. He might be a rock 'n' roll star, but his music was of the hip, intellectual variety. The Bob Dylan of a whole different generation. He'd survived one decade and moved successfully into another while his contemporaries had fallen by the wayside. His oldest music was now retro hip while his newest stuff won critical acclaim, and that kind of success impressed her. She knew it was as tough to be taken seriously in the music business of the post-MTV generation as it was to be taken seriously in the film industry. So in some ways, Romero had the kind of career she longed for.

When he'd paid attention to her—told her that her portrayal of a music groupie turned muse was inspired—she'd practically swooned at his feet. He saw the kind of talent in her that she wanted to have.

"That doesn't make it right." His voice was suddenly hard, and although she wanted to ask him why he'd gotten involved with her in the first place, she held her tongue.

She suspected she'd gotten all the relationship talk out of him that she would tonight. Changing the subject, she figured she would address a more immediate concern.

"Can I ask you something?"

"Shoot."

"How did you handle the loneliness on the road?"

In the distance a coyote howled, echoing the hollowness she felt inside even with Romero right next to her. She tried to think about the bits of sand clinging to the carpet and itching patches of bare skin, instead of the allure of a man she'd never been able to resist. She'd missed him so much these past few months.

"Are you kidding? I couldn't wait to be alone at the end of the day after twenty thousand people wanting a piece of me on any given night."

"I mean after you slide between your sheets at night." Her cheeks flushed warm at having to spell it out. "How do you deal with *that* kind of loneliness?"

She couldn't imagine falling asleep with this kind of ache inside her.

"Ah. Same way every guy does." He said it like the answer should have been self-evident.

"But you're not every guy. You're a rock star."

"So I'm not allowed to…engage in self-fulfillment? I don't get what you're driving at."

"According to every episode I've ever seen of *Behind the Music,* rock stars on the road have their choice of women hand-delivered to their room after a show." She'd swallowed back the question too many times during their relationship so that Romero wouldn't think she was insecure. But now that they'd broken up, what did it matter?

"And you buy that crap?" His hand shifted to her hip to push her back a few inches, as if to meet her gaze in the dark. The hints of moon coming through the opening of the shelter didn't give away enough of his expression. "That's no better than the film industry thinking you would sleep your way to the top just because the media says your mother did."

The comparison made sense. And yet…doubt niggled.

"But you've had the benefit of seeing how I conduct myself in Hollywood. I don't know anything about what your life is like on tour." The fact that he'd closed off his world to her had always hurt. "Whenever you've spent time with me on the road you've made sure to fly us to a neutral location."

Almost like he wanted to hide her.

Or maybe he'd just wanted to keep that whole side of his life all to himself.

"Because I was trying to shelter you from the mayhem of the foreign media, fighting band members and roadies still puking their guts out at eight in the morning from the night before." Romero's grip on her arm tightened. "Do you mean to tell me you've been thinking I might be sleeping with random women all this time? Why the hell didn't you just show up on-site if you were worried?"

"Because you never invited me." She tried to shrug as if it didn't matter, but her body felt stiff. Tense. "You always made a point of saying how cool it was that I didn't just show up unannounced, like every other clingy, awful ex-girlfriend you ever had. So I figured if you wanted me there, you would have asked."

Silence stretched.

"You needed an invitation?" His voice took on a softer note, and something about the tone made her feel silly somehow for bringing the whole thing up.

"I don't believe in going where I'm not wanted." She'd tried that once with her mother and the results had been ugly. "Thanks for the tip on handling the loneliness. I'll have to keep that in mind now that I'll be sleeping alone."

"You're not alone now." Romero's hand palmed her back and smoothed up her spine to massage her shoulder. "If you want an invitation, lady, you've got it. I'd be more than happy to make you forget everything about this day from hell if you'll let me."

Blood thrummed in Romero's temples, urging his fingers down her leg to the bare skin of her thigh.

"Romero?" Her voice was a thready whisper in the dark.

"Let me," he coaxed, knowing her pride would never allow her to ask him for more after he'd been the one to leave the home they'd made together. If he wanted to be with her tonight—and he wanted that so badly his whole body hurt—he'd need to make the first move.

"I've never…done anything like this outside a committed relationship." She didn't move an inch to either dissuade or encourage his caress, but he could feel the rapid beat of her pulse through her veins everywhere that he touched her.

"Shannon." He whispered her name, hearing the hunger in his voice that he couldn't have tamped down if he tried. "Don't you think I know that better than anyone? I might not have known everything you needed, but I know a lot about what you want. We moved in together a few weeks after we met just so you'd find out how damn committed I was."

More committed than he'd ever been. More crazy for her than anyone else.

He lowered his mouth to her shoulder where the T-shirt had eased down one arm. He nipped her bare skin and then grazed the spot with his tongue. The scent of hotel soap clung to her, mingling with the sweeter fragrance of her regular perfume and shampoo, which lingered in her hair. He wanted to inhale every bit of that scent on her, imprint it on his brain so he would never forget the potent effect she had on him.

Trailing his hand down the front of her thigh, he pushed the T-shirt away from her hip, exposing her sex to his touch. If only she would say the word...

"I want this so much," she whispered, her voice so soft he almost didn't catch it as he trailed kisses up her throat.

Her heartbeat pounded in her neck beneath his lips, her response growing palpable. He shifted his palm down her thighs, closing in on the place he wanted to touch most, pausing now to claim a tender patch of skin to stroke.

"I wouldn't hurt you." He hadn't meant to three months ago, and he'd be more careful now. "I don't have any protection anyway, but I can take the edge off if you let me."

He traced a circle on her skin, drawing out a pattern that he knew would please her if he transplanted the touch somewhere else. And if that was using insider information to get his own way, well, damn it, he wasn't the only one who would benefit.

"Yesss." Her affirmative hissed out between her teeth, and her body arched against his. Her head tipped forward to rest on his shoulder, her neck all the more exposed. Her long hair slid over his arm and down his back, a silky caress that sent a chill across his overheated skin.

Claiming another inch of skin inside her leg, Romero moved closer to her feminine heat.

"I've missed this. I've missed you," he admitted, transplanting his touch to the damp heat of her.

Her moan was the sweetest music he'd ever called from any instrument. He pressed the heel of his hand against her mound, her juices drenching him. She lifted her arms and wrapped them around his neck, a position of sweet surrender.

"Romero…" She started a soft chant of his name, an encore call for the best part of the time they'd shared together.

He throbbed to be inside her, her hips rocking urgently against him while his fingers played over her slick cleft.

Feeling that wetness, knowing how badly she wanted him, gave a knockout punch to all restraint. He plunged a finger within her and she covered his lips with hers, kissing him with unbridled hunger. His brain forgot everything else but her and this moment. Winding an arm around her back, he steadied her hips before easing another finger into her tight warmth. She hummed with pleasure, her legs squeezing against his hand even as she set up a rhythm to work herself over his touch.

By all that was holy, he wanted more of him inside her. He didn't have any protection, and she hadn't been on the Pill the whole time they'd been together. Hell, he'd purposely left his condoms at home for this trip to remind himself he couldn't go knocking on Shannon's door in the middle of the night, no matter how strong the urge to be in her bed.

He'd never imagined he'd be sleeping with her spooned against him in the middle of the desert, where there was nothing to distract him from how much he still wanted her.

Too soon, he felt her muscles tighten, her whole body tense. He bent to her breast and licked one taut nipple, tugging the crest into his mouth just as an orgasm swamped her. Wave after wave of spasms shook her, the aftershocks pulsing through her long after the bigger sensations had quieted.

There was nothing quiet about how he felt.

"Romero," Shannon mumbled, her mouth barely moving as she slumped into his chest. "Let me touch you."

Her fingers strayed down his abs, but he pulled his hips back.

"I don't know if I can handle that and not finish what we start."

She must have understood what he meant, since her fingers halted before sliding off him to rest harmlessly at her side.

"Are you sure?" She raised her head, meeting his gaze in the darkness, and even in the shadows he could see she was exhausted.

Then there was that head injury. The cuts on her hands. He needed to take care of her, not demand more.

"I'm sure." He stroked her hair and knew that he wouldn't have any trouble sleeping despite his hunger for her making his insides ache. At least tonight he had her back in his arms where she belonged.

The next thing he knew, Shannon's breathing had turned into the soft sounds of sleep, her inhalations rhythmic and deep.

In spite of his own needs, he would go to sleep grateful for having the chance to touch her. Had it been wise? Or had he only made it that much tougher to go back to their separate lives once they returned home? Their fighting cut too deeply for him to live through a repeat performance of three months ago, especially after growing up in a household full of constant bickering and unrealized dreams. But considering the way he and Shannon were getting close all over again, he feared he'd only set them both up for another heartache.

8

SHANNON STEPPED CAREFULLY through the desert at dawn, her fingers frozen and her breath huffing out in white clouds in front of her, even though the sun promised to warm things up soon.

Her feet protested every time they hit the cold desert sand. Her heart protested every time she thought about trying to resurrect some kind of boundary with Romero today. Last night had been amazing. Not just the intense physical satisfaction, which had always been a given with him. But because of what he'd confessed to her. That she had deserved better than him walking away.

Tears stung her eyes at the thought of what they'd lost, and she was thankful for the cold air that kept the tears from falling as she brushed her teeth and spat her toothpaste into the sand behind a tall organ pipe cactus. Shoving the tube back in her cosmetic bag, she trekked toward the fire pit from the night before, wondering how they would relate to one another today. She'd thought about waking him up with her hands all over him, but had dismissed the move as unfair, since he'd discouraged her from touching him the night before. She wouldn't take what he didn't want to give her freely. She never had.

With a sigh, she slumped down on a flat rock near the remains of the fire, her belly growling from hunger and her chest sore with the knowledge Romero might care for her enough to take her sexual itch away last night, but not enough to tread back into relationship waters with her.

A shuffling noise in the distance startled her. An animal?

There weren't that many places for a large animal to hide, with so much barren openness. But here and there sizable cacti dotted the landscape, large enough for a coyote. A bobcat.

Headhunters?

Suddenly paranoid, Shannon stood, backing away from the fire pit to seek shelter inside the lean-to.

"Romero," she whispered, still keeping an ear out for more noise. "I hear something."

When he didn't respond, she took her eyes off the desert to look at him.

He was gone.

At the same moment, more rustling came from somewhere outside, and she thought she saw the figure of a man darting behind a fat barrel cactus. Well, a leg and an arm maybe.

"Romero?" she called, hoping the shadow she'd seen had been his.

Even though he'd been wearing jeans so faded they'd never appear dark blue to a woman who could distinguish chartreuse from citron across an intimate gathering of two thousand.

Could it be someone else? A stranger?

"Hey!" she shouted, hoping the guy wasn't some psycho, and could help them out of the desert. "Over here!"

She started forward, but then caution got the best of her. Peering around for a stick, she grabbed a half-burned branch from the fire pit to use as protection just in case. But before she could set off toward the dense cluster of cactus to the west, she spied movement in the other direction.

Romero.

She wanted to call to him, to get his attention so he could help her corral the shadow form she thought she'd seen. But Romero was too far away and she could no longer spot the other man.

Had he been a mirage? Wishful thinking on her part? She squinted through the dawn light, to no avail.

Damn. Damn. Damn.

Turning back to Romero, she raised her arm to wave him over. He stalked silently toward her, his dark hair combed and his shirt changed from yesterday. He must have been out washing up, the same time as her. She looked back to the place where she'd thought she'd seen something. Heard something.

But there was no movement. Only quiet.

"Morning." Romero called to her from the other side of the wide desert valley.

She lifted her hand in greeting, not sure a shout would reach his ears, they were so far apart. Unlike Romero, she didn't possess a stage performer's lung capacity. Her voice was more Marilyn Monroe than Christina Aguilera.

"How committed are you to the vegan thing when

you're lost in the desert?" His long legs covered the terrain quickly, his voice getting louder as he closed the space between them.

She gave up looking for the shadow in the other direction, and dropped her stick to her side.

"Very." Even if she hadn't been a vegan, she had no desire to eat lizards or any of the other weirdo stuff like on a *Survivor* episode.

"Even if the alternative is starvation?"

"I don't think we need to worry about starving yet, do you? We've been lost less than twenty-four hours and we have those granola bars you'd stashed in the car." She took her cues from him and kept the conversation light. Avoiding the subjects that weighed on her heart today. Still, she had to share what she'd just seen. "You'll never guess what I saw when I was waiting for you to get back just now. A man."

"You what?"

"I saw—well, I think I saw—the shadow of a man slipping behind a cactus." She stuffed her cosmetic bag back in her luggage while Romero disassembled the shelter he'd made the night before.

"Where?" His frown made her suspect he thought she was crazy.

"Over there. Behind that big barrel cactus." She pointed, and her arm savored the slight warmth of the sun, which had popped up fully above the horizon. The morning remained cool, but she had a feeling she would stop shivering soon.

Without another word, Romero jogged to the spot she'd indicated, his five-o'clock shadow and stark expression making him look more like an action hero than a tabloid icon.

"Come here," he called, waving her over.

She zipped up her travel bag and hurried to see what he wanted. The cactus was farther away than it looked by one of those optical tricks of the desert.

"Don't tell me," she huffed, not because she was out of shape, but because her feet were in major pain after limping all that way. "You found a couple of branches that resemble a guy's legs, and want to rub it in that my eyesight stinks?"

"Nope." He pointed to the sand.

Two partial footprints remained.

"THERE REALLY WAS somebody here." Shannon looked as surprised as he felt. He'd figured she had mistaken an animal for a human, but the tracks in the sand told him differently. Someone had been close by.

"I don't think they could have been made before the rain yesterday." He knelt for a closer look, trying to see what direction they led.

"The rain would have washed them away." She peered around the cactus, careful not to get too close to the prints. "But those are the only ones I see. How could someone stand here and then disappear?"

"The ground is still a little damp near the root system, but dries out as you get away from it. The sands have shifted to cover any other tracks."

"So someone was here?"

"You said you saw him. Why didn't you flag him down? Ask him where the next town might be or if he knew of a quicker route?"

"I tried, but I thought it might be a desert mirage or something. Besides, the sun wasn't fully up, he was far away and I don't think he heard me. I could have used your vocal cords, but you were nowhere to be found." She folded her arms, having somehow turned the tables on Romero.

As if *he'd* been the one to let a possible escape out of their desert hell slip through his fingers. Not that all of last night had been hell. Just the part that involved staying away from her to save the sanity of them both. He'd hardly slept, and the unused testosterone stockpile would screw with his head for the next twenty-four hours.

Today promised to be an effing picnic.

"Well, since we have no clue what direction this guy headed after he left, we might as well stick to our course." He made a mental note of the boot imprint and a rough estimate of the shoe size—ten, probably—then stood. "You ready to get a move on?"

She snapped a salute and spun on her heel with only a small wince, her smart-ass attitude no doubt intended to show him he was being…something. Pushy, insensitive, unfeeling.

He was just glad to gain a few feet of distance from her so he could think again, without the distraction of her breasts in his old Ramones T-shirt. The woman was killing him, even if she at least had her jeans back on today.

It wasn't until they were packed up and ready to leave the campsite that he realized he'd never said anything to her about the night before. About how much it meant to him to touch her. Or how much he was starting to wonder if their breakup had been a huge mistake.

All of which he'd planned to cover before getting

sidetracked by the discovery they weren't alone in the desert. But then, conversation had never been his strong suit, especially when it came to discussing *them*. Maybe he'd just have to show her they were meant to be together.

"Tell me more about the script."

Romero figured talking about her work was as good a place to start as any. He'd gotten so involved in his own during those months before their split that he'd neglected to ask her much about hers. He regretted that, since her commitment to acting was something he admired. And even if he didn't always agree with her creative choices, he liked that she had a vision for herself and worked hard not to follow in anyone else's footsteps. Shannon forged her own path.

They'd been walking for about an hour since breaking camp, and instead of making inroads with Shannon, he'd only managed to inventory all the ways he'd failed this woman. Like a movie reel in constant rewind, his thoughts kept going back to what she would do in Hollywood now if she didn't take the *Baby Doll* movie. Would she even be able to afford half of the house if she wanted to buy him out?

She loved that place, and he hated to think of her living anywhere else.

But she hadn't said anything about that. How many times during their relationship had she hidden her own worries and he'd never noticed? It didn't settle well with him to think he might have something in common with her self-absorbed mother.

"What's there to tell?"

He could see her shrug from his position a few feet

behind her. Her shoulders rose and fell in a quick, sinuous movement. Pieces of hair escaped the knot at her nape, the long strands brushing her back and outlining the vulnerable column of her neck.

They hadn't seen anything outside of cacti and scrub all morning, the sea of dull green against a brown backdrop unbroken by anything except themselves.

"You said it was better than you expected, but I'm surprised you even had it with you, considering how against it you were." He remembered that much at least, even if he'd tuned out anything else she might have mentioned about it a few months ago. Trying to come up with material for a new album had been all-consuming during that time.

The creative process didn't get easier the longer you were in the business. It got tougher. He knew how many ways he could fail, and how much critics would love to shred his efforts. After all, panning the work of an artist who was a commercial success brought a music reviewer a hell of a lot more attention than writing off some new band no one had ever heard of before.

"I don't have any firm plans for my next project," she hedged, darting around his comment in a way that struck him as unusual for a woman who didn't mind voicing her opinions.

"What else are you considering?" Again, he felt the sting of guilt that he didn't even *know* what other options she was looking at for future work.

She'd accused him of being so wrapped up in his music that he ignored everything else around him, but he'd rejected the idea, telling himself that he'd seen her far more than when he'd been on tour. But maybe sitting his ass in the same house as her didn't mean he'd been paying attention.

"I don't know." She paused to run her finger over the red flower of a blooming cactus. "I thought about doing something really different."

"Stand-up comedy?" He couldn't imagine what she had in mind, but had no doubt she'd be good at anything she tried.

He sidestepped a scraggly little Christmas cactus.

"Actually, I'm thinking about taking some time off from Hollywood and doing some theater."

He halted. It took him a half a minute before he realized he needed to keep moving.

"Theater?"

She couldn't have surprised him more if she'd announced she'd been abducted by aliens. And carried a Martian's baby as a result.

"Yes." Her reply was clipped.

Maybe those Martians had made off with his opinionated ex-girlfriend and left a quiet stranger in her place. How could she give up on her biggest professional dreams?

"I thought you hated the theater." He remembered her stories about a season of summer stock in New England and how much she'd disliked the overdramatic nature of it. "Too stuffy and pretentious. Wait a minute."

He halted midstep and reached out to stop her, too.

She whirled to face him, the knot at the back of her head listing to the right as she did so. "What?"

"Do you mean New York theater? As in moving three thousand miles away?" He'd never sent a woman run-

ning that far, and he'd had some powerfully bad break-
ups in his day.

His chest tightened at the idea of Shannon so out
of his reach.

"If I decide to tackle the theater, yes, it will be in New
York." Her voice remained cool and calm. Detached.

And, damn it, he felt as if she'd just ripped the rug
out from under his feet.

"You've never had any interest in theater before." He
released her arm to rub his hand across his chest, right
where the squeezing sensation resided. "Are you doing
this just to get away from me?"

9

"OF COURSE NOT." Shannon turned away from him, needing to keep walking before this conversation tread any closer to her plans for her future. She didn't need for Romero to know her life was falling apart completely. "I just thought this would be a good time to explore something new."

"But why theater when you don't like it?" he asked a minute later, his voice trailing after her along with his footsteps. "If you want to try something new, work on a TV sitcom. You don't need to go all the way to New York."

"What do you—"

A thunderous animal roar cut her off.

She stopped in her tracks and tried her hardest not to wet herself. The growl dropped into a low, threatening rumble, an extended warning that seemed to vibrate the ground all around them.

"It's okay," Romero whispered from behind her, his body suddenly a mere inch away. "Don't move, but see if you can spot where it came from."

Another full-blown roar split the air, louder this time. The hair on her neck stood up. She'd never heard a sound like that outside of a zoo, and possibly not even there.

"I see it." Romero pointed to a brown lump on top

of a large, flat rock a few hundred meters away. "We'll just keep moving and make lots of noise."

A mountain lion stared back at them from its perch, shoulders flexing as the beast appeared ready to spring.

Shannon's throat dried up, her heart slamming so fast she thought it might burst from overexertion. Romero nudged her forward but her feet were glued to the earth.

"We shouldn't play dead?" She thought slinking away seemed smarter than making a racket, but Romero was already waving his hands in the air.

"Hell, no. That thing will be on you in no time if he thinks he can take you." He shoved her more forcefully this time. "Come on."

Shannon forced herself to sidestep away from the full-grown cat, keeping her eyes on Simba the whole time.

"Getting mauled would be an awful way to die," she whispered, partly because she was so scared and partly because her vocal cords were under major duress along with the rest of her.

"Nobody's dying today," Romero assured her. "Stomp your feet and get moving. As long as that animal knows we're too big for him to manage easily, he'll go right back to whatever he was doing before we got here."

Reluctantly, Shannon set her feet in motion a little faster.

No mauling, no mauling, no mauling. Please, no mauling.

"He looks hungry," she observed, noting the way the animal's shoulder bones were prominent through its sandy-colored fur. "Like he hasn't had a meal in weeks."

"Probably why he's protective of his territory," Romero answered in a loud voice, sticking by his idea that making noise was a good thing. "He can't afford any competition if the food sources are scarce."

"Ha!" Her voice still didn't have full power so the sound came out as cracked and parched as the desert around them. None of the rest of her had much juice, either. Her legs felt as if they'd wobble right out from underneath her. "I'm thinking we look more like the food source than the competition."

The cat didn't seem to be following them, although it paced along its rock outcropping with a wary eye and watched them move to the north instead of east, the way they had been going.

"Nope. If we were alone, we might look like a food source, but a cat like that doesn't usually go after a group."

"We're only one person removed from being alone." Shannon picked up speed as she realized the animal was staying put. As far as she was concerned, the more distance between her and the starving feline, the better.

"And that's enough. All the more reason why you shouldn't take off alone anymore." His feet hit the ground with excessive force, making her realize how quietly he normally moved. He'd also scooped up a long branch of dead brush at some point, and brandished the thing like a weapon.

"I don't plan on having to stay in this desert for another night." She'd never hold back a second night in Romero's arms. Even now, with the threat of a mountain lion behind them and some weirdo desert dweller trailing them, Shannon still wanted to plaster herself to this man and remind him how good they were together.

"You're looking at this all wrong." He made an expansive gesture with his hand; the branch he carried swept the horizon. "You know how many people would love the chance to experience the most beautiful desert in the world like this? Firsthand and not through some cheesy safari tour?"

"That's right. I love walking on broken high heels until blisters form, sleeping on a scrap of car upholstery and getting chased by mountain lions. What was I thinking?" She purposely downplayed all that was wonderful about being alone with him as she watched the catamount pace its rock ledge a few more times before lying down again, apparently satisfied to let them pass.

Thank the saints.

"Think about it." Romero's gaze slid over to hers now that the threat of being devoured had subsided. "We've got careers that allow us to make our own schedules, and an opportunity to take some downtime for sightseeing. I call that good fortune."

Perhaps *he* had a job that let him take some downtime. She was on the verge of bankruptcy if she didn't nail down her next engagement soon. Oh, and she was days away from homelessness, since she couldn't afford to make his half of the mortgage payments to the bank, and she sure as heck couldn't swing buying him out. None of which she felt like sharing with a man who'd never failed at anything except a lasting relationship.

Saying nothing, she peered back toward the puma and realized how totally out of her element she was here. Romero might be adapting just fine, but her brand of resourcefulness was a far cry from his. She navigated press junkets and award ceremonies, charity balls and red-carpet premieres, not sand dunes and wildlife encounters.

Was this how her mother had felt in Hollywood? A small-town girl whose fame grew too fast for her to process, Bridget Leigh had never really understood Tinseltown. She'd been dragged over its rough terrain by her natural blond roots thanks to managers, producers and directors who'd all wanted to cash in on her rising star. Until, eventually, she'd encountered the fattest predator ever to work Melrose Avenue—drug addiction.

At least out here, identifying the enemy was easy. Well, the four-legged variety anyway. Shannon didn't want to think about the dangers inherent in feeling too comfortable with her walking companion.

"Shan?" Romero slowed down beside her, his hand snaking lightly around her waist. "I'd get you home if I could."

His dark eyes locked on hers and a dangerous flutter stirred in her belly. It would be so easy to be drawn back into his life. His world.

"I know." She disengaged herself from his touch, since she hadn't exactly grown immune to his charm. Take last night. She would have tossed her pride aside like a used dust rag if he'd shown any interest in taking their heated game to the next level, especially since she had a few condoms of her own saved up for a rainy day.

If she stuck around him much longer, she would surely beg him to put them to good use with her.

"Can I only touch you at night?"

His voice wound around her with all its seductive possibilities, reminding her of the songs he'd written about her. About them. How could she explain to him how much it hurt to be drawn into a relationship he didn't take as seriously as she did? Maybe if her career had been on a firm footing. Or her financial situation. But her whole world was unstable, and having her emotions played with, too—even if that's not what he intended—was more than she could handle.

"Do you know why I always try to appear together in public? For the cameras?" She paused, turning to meet his gaze. "Because I'm not that confident. I need to assemble myself carefully, like an armor to protect myself from the world. That's how it is with you, too. I just can't…open myself to the sting."

Ignoring the furrowed lines on his forehead and other signs of confusion, she turned and kept on walking.

"Can I ask you one other thing?"

She paused. Nodded.

"Why do you want to fight all the time?"

The question hung in the air like a bad smell. Hadn't he paid attention to any disagreement they'd ever had?

"I *don't* like to fight all the time." She couldn't even see the cat anymore, but her eyes were more alert now, seeking out other patches of brown fur on the dusty landscape. "I like to discuss issues before they turn into problems, and work through them. Ideally, I'd like to do that frequently—discuss and solve. That way you understand each other better and fix little things before they become insurmountable."

Weariness crept through her even though the day couldn't have progressed much past noon. Revisiting old ground made her feel more caked in mud than she had during the rain yesterday.

"Discussion without the boxing gloves." His expression seemed thoughtful. As if he'd just had a major revelation.

"I guess so. Yes. I think there's a lot of benefits to airing disagreements." She trudged onward, the cuffs of her jeans kicking up dust as she patted her throat to be sure her mother's necklace still hung around her neck. "Assuming *both* parties engage in the process."

A noncommittal grunt sounded from behind her before Romero cleared his throat.

"The problem is, I don't like to argue."

SHANNON SURPRISED HIM when she laughed. She stepped closer to him, within touching distance.

"Do you think your aversion to arguing is news to me?"

"I don't know." He shrugged, not remembering how much he'd told her about that. "I always hated the noise and the arguing at my house, growing up. My brothers could never get it through their heads that I was wired differently than they were. My family took out their anger physically. Verbally. I picked up a guitar."

She stood so close to him he couldn't help feeling as if they were the only two people in the world right now. What was to stop them from taking advantage of this time together? They'd always understood each other sexually.

And all the arguing or lack of arguing in the world hadn't changed that. Without weighing the costs of his action, he pulled her into the circle of his arms. Hands bracketing her hips, he leaned in to kiss her, savoring the way her eyes widened and her mouth went slack with surprise.

Desire.

He kissed her there, right on those full lips, teasing his tongue across their glossy sweetness. She held back for a moment, but he was not having any of it. If she wanted out of this kiss, she could damn well start her infernal arguing right now, because this was one thing he'd go to the mat for. One thing they hadn't polluted with pointless fights that left them exhausted.

Aligning his hips with hers, he pressed closer. She gripped his shoulders with sudden fierceness, obviously getting the message. Her breasts molded to his chest.

Her hips cradled his, the heat of her apparent right through two layers of denim. If she'd been wearing a skirt, he would have been inside her already.

He bent to kiss the side of her throat, nipping a spot guaranteed to make her shiver with need. He'd never met a woman with such a sensitive neck.

A shudder rippled through her, ending in a slight roll of her hips that set off a fresh ache to be buried deep in her.

"This isn't fighting fair," she murmured, even as her neck arched to give him better access.

Her thighs gave way, removing another barrier from where he wanted to be as he shifted his leg between hers. She bit off a sweet sigh of pleasure, but not before he'd heard the first sexy notes.

"Sweetheart, this isn't fighting at all. That's my whole point."

She tightened her grip on his shirt, her fingernails grazing his shoulders through the cotton. And didn't that bring back memories? He'd found telltale crescent moon marks in those same exact places before.

He blew on the damp spot on her neck where he'd kissed her. Her eyelids fluttered but didn't close.

"But did you bring condoms out into the desert with you?"

The question stopped him short. The breath he'd been exhaling along her flesh dried up, since he hadn't thought that far ahead.

"I don't want to tease you. Or me either, for that matter." She wriggled away from him a few inches. "And since we didn't plan on getting back together, maybe we shouldn't be indulging ourselves without thinking through what it means."

With regret, he released her. She had a point.

"She's killing me," he informed no one in particular as he willed his body back into submission.

He'd stopped last night, but he didn't know how much longer he could count on that noble streak if he and Shannon continued to be in close proximity. Condom or no condom, he was damn tempted to override all sense of caution and remind his ex-girlfriend of everything they were giving up.

And wasn't that one hell of a surprise for a guy who'd never had trouble walking away from a woman?

"Unbelievable." Shannon shook her head as she picked up her fallen overnight bag and thrust her arm through the strap.

"What?" He didn't think his brain cells would be functioning anytime soon, what with his attention being preoccupied by thwarted sex and too much self-realization for his peace of mind.

"You're not the least bit intimidated by the sight of a ravenous mountain lion in the wild, but the thought of discussing our relationship sends you into full-fledged panic."

Romero didn't have a damn thing to say in return, and for once, it wasn't only because he didn't want to argue. This time, it just so happened he couldn't agree more.

10

THANKFULLY, Romero didn't know about the trio of condoms stashed in her travel bag.

Their presence revealed a secret optimism Shannon was embarrassed to admit feeling when she'd packed for the wedding. Sure, she'd settled into life without him, but after three months, she'd had plenty of time to miss him. As the rest of her friends prepared for Valentine's Day with their significant others, Shannon had hoped maybe Amy's romantic nuptials would inspire equally romantic thoughts in her ex.

It had been a foolish wish, she realized. Romero hadn't paid much attention to her at the wedding outside of the obligatory dance, and offering a ride home when her travel plans fell through. And by now she knew he didn't see their lack of communication as an obstacle the way she did. Well, maybe he saw the obstacle in a peripheral way, since he'd apologized for their big blowup. But he'd never suggested he would do anything differently in the future. Or that he wished they had another shot at it.

Now, as she trudged just ahead of him on her tired, sore feet, she struggled to focus on the surprising beauty of her stark surroundings instead of the sexy aura of the man behind her.

And, yes, he had an aura. She'd never bought into a lot of post-hippie West Coast thinking, but she believed that an invisible energy surrounded every person. How else did she know whenever Romero Jinks walked into a room long before she saw him with her own eyes? And what else could explain the subtle pulse of sexual attraction in the air when she couldn't even see a smidge of the six-foot-two stud in jeans a few yards away? The man exuded chemistry through his damn pores.

"Is it just me, or are we going uphill?" She had to break the silence that had been dogging them since her last outbreak of none-too-subtle accusation.

If she had any sense, she'd quit falling into his arms and returning to the source of their old problems, but it wasn't easy being isolated with him when she missed him. Missed *them* as a couple. She needed a distraction or she'd lose her marbles.

"It's not just you," he replied, his slow response suggesting he'd been preoccupied, as if his thoughts were a million miles away. Was he already thinking about his next concert tour? Future trips to Catalina without her?

Maybe once she moved to New York, she wouldn't miss him so much because she wouldn't be tripping over their old friends or living in the house they'd once shared. The notion failed to cheer her and, in fact, only served to depress her further.

"Do you think it's strange that we haven't reached a highway or seen a hint of civilization in all the time we've been walking?" She didn't count the brief sighting of the phantom man behind the cactus as an encounter with someone "civilized," since he had ignored her shout and left them to fend for themselves with a mountain lion.

"Not really." As they worked their way northeast, he thumped a long walking stick on the sandy ground to warn off snakes and other wild beasts. "There are large tracts of undeveloped land down here and we haven't covered that much ground on foot. When you're in a car, you don't get a real handle on how many barren miles you're crossing because you're moving through it so much faster."

Worry clamped cold teeth around her. "I told Ceily I'd be home yesterday, so she didn't need to worry about feeding the dogs." Her two Pekingese-Chihuahua mixes would be lonely and starving by the time she came home. Would they think she'd abandoned them?

He scrubbed a hand over her shoulder. "They probably started howling ten minutes after dinnertime. How much you want to bet Mrs. Norbitz has already been over there with leftovers for them?"

Their neighbor was a fifty-year-old divorcee who loved to cook but couldn't eat any of her meals due to a perpetual diet to maintain her hundred-pound frame. She also bred poodles—as inconspicuously as possible so as not to get in trouble with local dog ordinances, since there was a limit on the number of animals per household.

And for a career woman who'd known the score with Romero all along, Shannon sure had gotten friendly with the neighbors, hadn't she? Maybe she'd nested in that big Hollywood Hills house more than she'd realized.

"I think we scared her off from using her key ever since she walked in on us while we were testing out the new couch." Still, Shannon appreciated his effort to reassure her. And the dogs had sniffed out the bag of food in the laundry room a couple of times when she'd been tardy with dinner, so surely they would help themselves with a bit of pawing and gnawing of the paper sack.

"I would hope the sound of the dogs howling would be a far cry from the noises you make during sex."

Pausing to shoot Romero a glare, Shannon marveled that he could tease her and get her thinking about sex all at the same time. Lord, protect her from a man with that much magnetism.

They'd christened that new couch the same way they had christened every other piece of furniture they had bought together. Romero had said if it wasn't comfortable enough to accommodate the occasional tryst, it didn't have any business in their house.

"I'm sure she would be able to distinguish the two. My point is that I don't think she'll be so quick to let herself in anymore, even if she's home this weekend." Thoughts of the dogs missing her helped Shannon shut out visions of what she could do with those three condoms she'd packed, if she'd been the kind of woman who took pleasure where she could find it instead of worrying about her heart.

"There are five bathrooms in that house, and you know one of them has a toilet seat up so they'll have water. And they can't starve in a day or even a couple of days without food." Romero reached to stroke her hair with his free hand, a gesture of tenderness she missed about him.

And, oh, God, why couldn't she just think about the plight of her dogs and not where things stood with Romero? Goose bumps on her arms from that simple stroke told her she wouldn't shake off memories of other touches and happier times together anytime soon.

Spinning on her heel, she put one foot in front of the other, determined to get away from him and their desert ordeal before she dug into her bag for those three condoms—three last chances for happiness.

"I'm sure you're right." Taking a deep breath, she caught a change in the air. Not necessarily a scent, but a feel of something different. "What's that?"

Stopping again, she inhaled deeply.

"What's what?" Romero halted alongside her, his warm, muscular body so close to hers their auras must be mingling.

At least that's the reason she gave herself for the sudden sensation of being engulfed in flames.

"The air feels different." Peering ahead, she spotted thicker foliage on as the terrain rose in front of them. "And the greenery is so dense up there."

"A cactus forest." He shifted his weight to lean on his walking stick, his denim-clad hip a mere inch from hers. "You'd better cover your arms to navigate through that stuff."

Little did he realize that if she had possessed heavier clothes she would have already been wearing them to protect herself from stray brushes of his arms. Of his warm, broad palms.

Damn her thoughts.

"Actually, I do have my satin blazer." She unzipped her bag to retrieve the garment. It already had blood and dirt stains that would never come out, so a few pulls in the fabric wouldn't hurt anything.

The extra layer of cloth might save her sanity around Romero. Reaching for the creamy material, she realized two things at the exact same time.

First, major contraband was stashed in the folds of the jacket, thanks to her crappy packing job. And second, Romero was eyeing her movements like a hawk.

Crap.

"What are you doing?" He stood over her, watching her frantically sort through the bag before she zipped it back up again, having accomplished exactly nothing.

She'd have to wait until he wasn't around to retrieve it.

"I…don't want to wreck the blazer," she lied, since she was flustered by the sight of the condoms and wasn't thinking straight. She tried to stuff a corner of the creamy fabric back into the bag, and had to unzip it again. "The satin is too thin to provide protection anyway. I'll just test out the cactus forest first and see if I'll be okay without it."

"Are you crazy?" He reached for the hint of ivory material still peeking out, and started to pull. "I'll wear it if you don't, Shan. Those needles will seriously tear up your skin."

Uh-oh.

"You're going to ruin it," she argued, her face flaming at the thought of him finding what she had stashed in there.

He tugged harder and all at once the bag coughed up its contents on the desert sand. Her few clothes spilled everywhere. Toiletries sprang out in disarray.

Along with three unused condoms wrapped in shiny foil.

HE'D OPENED PANDORA'S BOX.

Every emotion and possible reaction Romero might have seemed to float up from Shannon's carry-on along with her incriminating belongings. Anger that she'd lied by omission in not owning up to a condom stash. Hurt that she'd been so desperate to avoid intimacy she'd felt she couldn't be honest. And—against all reason—aroused at even the thought of sex being a possibility.

"I'm just going to assume you had me in mind when these found their way into your suitcase." He hadn't meant to blurt out the first thought that came to him, but there it was.

She froze, her movements to retrieve her things coming to an abrupt halt.

"You don't have to ask."

"How is my comment any different than you asking me if I was with the groupie the night after the wedding? You think I wasn't insulted then?" He realized how little she understood him, how their relationship had unraveled during months of miscommunication. But then, he'd always been better at working out his problems in his songs rather than in real life.

Her hand reached for the condoms on the ground between them and he stooped to catch her fingers in his.

"Not a chance," he warned her, keeping her hand imprisoned in his. "I'm going to be in charge of any and all condom usage this trip."

Scooping up the packets, he felt her pulse thrum beneath his thumb as he jammed the prophylactics into his shirt pocket with his other hand.

"Technically, they're mine." Her movements were jerky as she picked up the rest of her things—some soap inside a plastic bag, her brush and the hotel shampoo. Her cheeks had heated, the color crawling up her neck to flood her face the same way a good orgasm would.

He noticed she didn't touch the blazer.

He couldn't believe she'd packed those condoms. Knowing that she didn't believe in sex outside of a committed relationship, he had to think part of her wanted to get back together. No matter that she snipped at him. No matter that she'd packed all of his clothes when he'd suggested they separate for a while.

This changed everything.

"I'll, uh, make sure you get your money's worth out of them." He patted the pocket where he'd stashed the condoms, and cleared his throat, not sure what to make of this piece of news. He picked up the script for *Baby Doll* and flicked off some kind of sand beetle darting across the manila envelope. "Don't forget this."

She plucked at her blazer, which was still dragging on the ground, and drew it from his hand.

"I won't forget this, either. I know how much you wanted me to wear it." Jamming her arms into the sleeves, she stalked off toward the cactus forest.

Something about her retreating form limping across the harsh terrain stabbed at his conscience, making him regret the way he'd spoken to her. The way he'd commandeered the condoms. She obviously hadn't wanted him to know about them, and maybe she had good reason—a reason that still applied.

After all, she'd told him that sex wasn't a sound way to end an argument between two people. And she had a point. He'd been running hard and fast from this relationship and he'd never really stopped to consider why.

But as he watched her figure get smaller the farther

she moved from him, his chest tightened with that same ache he'd known after the car accident, when he'd been afraid she was hurt. What would the ache be like when she walked away from him forever, taking all her fiery ways and vibrant sexual energy with her?

A pit opened inside him, scaring him more than facing a desertful of poisonous snakes and feline predators. Going back to his old existence, the pre-Shannon one, might preserve the loner lifestyle he'd hammered out for himself as a rebel rock 'n' roller. But at what cost?

He wished he could make the roller-coaster ride stop long enough for him to think about that, but she was already disappearing into the desert forest—a sea of huge green cardon cacti that towered as tall as any normal trees. He needed to be there with her before she attracted trouble—a talent she had a knack for.

As he sprinted across the sand, grit worked its way into his shoes and rubbed his skin raw. He was still about a hundred yards behind when he heard her squeal and saw her stop short at the edge of the thicket.

A scorpion? Snake? If she got bitten, he didn't have a prayer of getting her to a hospital.

He shoved his bag off his shoulders and prepared to do battle with...

A pair of coyote pups wrestling and nipping one another, their tails wagging as they tumbled together in the universal pastime of siblings.

"Aren't they cute?" Shannon whispered to him, her whole expression transformed from the embarrassment of a few minutes ago. Now her gaze turned practically maternal as she knelt close to the fluffy pups.

"Bad idea, babe." He reached for her arm, hauling

her back up to her feet. "You know their mother can't be far off, and for all you know, she could reject these two if she smells you on them."

"Are coyotes like that?" She frowned for a moment until the dogs stopped to stare at her.

The animal with the lighter-colored fur had an ear that folded in half as he cocked his head to take their measure. Shannon cooed with dog-lover joy.

"I have no idea, but why risk it?" Romero couldn't deny a small piece of dog-lover in his own heart that wanted to scoop up the pups and cart them home. Those big, dark eyes would win over anyone.

Although possibly not border patrol.

"But I don't see the mother." Shannon peered around, biting her lower lip. "What if something happened to her and these little cuties are on their own?"

"Do those round bellies look neglected to you?" He gave her a nudge before he ended up carrying a dog for the next fifty miles. "Let's get going before we piss off another wild animal today, okay? Never underestimate the battle capabilities of a mother who thinks you're threatening her brood."

Shannon nodded reluctantly, her feet still not moving of their own accord.

"If I have to carry you, I guarantee I'm going to make it worth my while." He allowed his gaze to roam over her to stress his point.

And, whoa. That tactic was apt to backfire, since his body responded in a nanosecond.

Thankfully, she huffed something indignant at him and turned from the pups to move into the cactus thicket in a northeasterly direction. With any luck, they'd reach the highway soon, since the increasingly green terrain had to mean the Gulf of California or some other water source loomed nearby. Their time together would be at an end as soon as they could find that road and flag down a car.

That should have been welcome news given how badly Shannon wanted to get back to her dogs, her career and the new opportunities waiting for her in New York. Unfortunately, the longer Romero spent with her, the more he realized the only thing he had to go back to was the rock 'n' roll life of one tour after another. A chain of empty hotel rooms without the prospect of meeting Shannon in exotic cities to break up the monotony.

This survival trek in the desert was his last chance to figure out if he was going to be okay with that. Or if splitting from Shannon had been the worst mistake of his life.

"Do you hear something?" She turned around suddenly, her feet kicking up dust while her loosely bound hair swung in an arc away from her body.

He listened.

Harder.

"What?" Had standing in front of concert-quality amps for two decades taken a toll on his hearing?

"I thought I heard a car engine."

11

SHE HALF EXPECTED Romero to charge through the cactus thicket at hyperspeed to look for signs of the lost highway. So she was shocked when he waved off her observation.

"If we're close to a road, there will be another car along soon enough." He set down his overnight bag. "Right now, I want to apologize for what I said back there. I knew damn well you didn't pack protection for some random guy. I guess I just couldn't believe my luck that you might have had me in mind after all we've been through."

His hands found her shoulders and stroked over them lightly, rubbing down her arms and back up again.

And, oh, what a test to a woman's willpower to have him standing mere inches behind her. The urge to close her eyes and lean into him was so strong she thought she might be swaying on her feet.

Forcing herself to be absolutely still, she took shallow breaths while he tugged the collar of her blazer more snugly around her. With gentle hands he swept the back of her neck to free a few strands of trapped hair that had escaped the loose knot sagging listlessly to the right.

It was that tender thoughtfulness for her comfort that

did her in. Well, that and remembering how considerate he was of her body. Romero had a way of physically adoring her that could have become addictive. In fact, maybe she already was hooked and craving him, since her eyes quickly fell to half-mast and pleasure tumbled through her at his nearness.

"I can't even remember what it was like to be with anyone else," she whispered, unable to hold back anymore after three long months apart. Turning, she sank into his heat, wanting nothing so much as his touch.

Her body sang with need at the feel of his hard chest and the solid plank of his abs. He ran every day. The rigorous commitment gave him a bod many men left behind at twenty-five.

"I like hearing that." He twined his fingers through the knot in her hair and deftly unwound it from the clip she'd jammed in it that morning. "I feel exactly the same way, Shan."

Sunlight filtered through the giant green cacti, which softened its glare and wrapped them in their own private world. Sheltered from the dry winds and blowing sand, they remained hidden from any other creatures that might roam the desert.

Shannon's scalp tingled as he combed his fingers through her hair, his eyes focused on hers. Seeing inside her.

"I never wanted you to leave." She admitted the truth that had been too painful to confess at any other time.

"I never wanted to go." He pinched a lock and slid his thumb and finger down its length to just above her breasts, where the strands pooled. His knuckles traced the valley in between and she shivered at the contact.

Years of fretwork on the guitar had hardened his fingertips to layers of callus, but that had never affected their sensitivity, or his ability to intuit exactly how to touch her to bring her the most gratification.

"Really?" Pleasure warmed her as hope blossomed inside her.

Had Romero really started to appreciate that they had something good together? It wasn't much to resurrect a relationship on, but it was all she needed to justify touching him. Tasting him. Losing herself in him. She'd figure out what it all meant later, when feel-good hormones weren't bombarding her.

"I can't let you go, Shan." He smoothed away her hair, pushing it behind her shoulders so nothing stood between his hand and her chest except her T-shirt. "Not yet."

Her body hummed with awareness, her skin heating in anticipation of his touch. His kiss. She knew it was coming, but, oh, man, Romero liked taking his time.

She didn't like waiting for many things in life, but she'd been seduced by him often enough to know how well rewarded she would be if he proceeded at his own pace. No man had ever driven her to the kind of passionate highs that he could. Besides, he didn't want to let her go.

That right there was enough to make her want to stay lost in the desert with him.

His hands smoothed inside her blazer, across her collarbone and down her shoulders to her bare arms. Her breasts ached with the need for his touch, and a pathetic little cry leaped from her throat before she could suppress it. She didn't regret that noise so much when his fingers slipped under the hem of the shirt and cupped her waist, his thumbs playing over her stomach like a fine instrument.

The aching desire that plagued her breasts now bloomed between her hips. Like liquid fire, a rush of heat flooded her senses, and her body demanded contact with his.

"If you don't want me to tackle you into a cactus, you'd better start getting naked." Shannon tucked a finger in his belt and drew him closer, her hips leading the charge.

He chuckled softly, but didn't deny her. With easy movements he peeled the blazer off her shoulders and tossed it aside. Then he released her long enough to retrieve the wool blanket from his bag. With the snap of his wrists, it billowed out behind her. A ready-made bed.

When she turned to check out his work, he swept her feet out from under her and caught her in his arms, cradling her against him while he lowered her to the ground.

"Is that better?" He pinned her wrists above her head and lay stretched out over her for a long moment, letting her savor the feel of all that male heat and pressure.

"Yes." The nudge of a small stone in her lower back wasn't a problem with his thighs edging between hers, his arousal pressing at his jeans and making its presence known. "So, so much better."

She couldn't move much with him holding her down, so she settled for lifting her head to nip his lower lip. His eyes narrowed before his gaze slipped to her mouth, and she knew that even flat on her back, she had the upper hand for a moment. Refusing to waste it, she darted her tongue along her upper lip, tasting him there.

Romero tracked the movement with darkening eyes.

"It's been too long." His voice rasped with hunger.

They'd once had a pact never to go longer than one week without touching each other. They'd flown all over the world to honor that agreement, reuniting in nameless hotels and airports even if their schedules had allowed them only a few stolen hours together.

"We were already stretching the one-week limit when we broke up," she agreed, loving the way it felt to be this man's center of attention.

"Never again." He made the vow as if he meant it with his whole heart, and for now, no matter what the future held, she allowed herself to believe it.

"Touch me," she ordered, barely giving any sound to the words. He was close enough she could move her lips and he would know what she said. Especially given the way his eyes devoured her slightest movement.

He cupped her hip with a free hand and lowered his mouth to her breast. With unerring aim, he nipped the crest through the layer of her bra and T-shirt. Desire gnawed her belly and spurred her hips to roll against his. Releasing her hands, he skimmed off her shirt and breathed warm air onto the tight points. Her bra chafed her skin, making the ache worse until he peeled the lace down with his teeth.

Shivers raced over her flesh and she couldn't be still. She pulled him to her, needing the relief only his mouth could provide.

His lips closed over the tip and pleasure bolted through her. Her back arched and she searched wildly for the hem of his shirt, wanting him naked against her.

"Oh, please," she murmured, his name a constant on her tongue as she sang out a litany of praise for what he made her feel.

His skill was immeasurable as he swirled his tongue around the crest of her nipple and unsnapped her jeans. Her breath whooshed through her lungs in great gulps.

"I dreamed about this all night," he admitted, his own breath fanning across her stomach as he kissed his way down her torso.

"I would have taken the edge off for you." She unfastened his jeans and stroked his shaft through his boxers. "Remember?"

He covered her palm with his, halting her fingers in midexploration.

"That offer was half the reason I couldn't stop thinking about you." He plucked her hand off him and placed it on his chest. "So unless you want the fastest performance you've ever seen, I suggest you let me set the pace."

"But I need you inside me." She didn't like the whimper in her voice, but some things in life were unavoidable.

He pushed her jeans off her hips and managed to get his most of the way off before she found a condom in his shirt pocket.

With a low groan he took it and, tearing open the packet with his teeth, rolled it on. She hitched at her panties, trying to work herself out of them while still underneath him, but he took over that job, too, his mouth fastening on her breast while he dragged her underwear down her legs and off.

Now, naked except for the bra that no longer covered her, Shannon rubbed herself against him shamelessly, absorbing the feel of his hot skin. His muscles flexed and jumped in response, his cock nudging the dampness between her thighs.

"Shannon." He released her nipple and gazed down into her eyes as he slid a finger inside her.

Her hands flexed and clawed lightly against his skin, her body tightening around him as he worked her with one finger and then two. Her slick heat eased his touches, her body so ready for him she thought she would explode.

Tension coiled inside her and she spread her legs wider. Inviting. Only then did he withdraw his fingers to taste her wetness. He took obvious pleasure in savoring her that way, his groan raking across her senses while her body craved more of him. It only took one small whimper from her to encourage him. Positioning himself between her legs, he plunged his cock deep inside her.

The earth moved.

Time stopped.

She thought the heavens probably opened up, but she couldn't see past the cactus branches overhead. Romero filled her so completely she let out a cry to rival any wild animal's. Lifting up, she tested his shoulder with her teeth and wrapped her legs around his waist. Her ankles locked above his taut butt as his muscles worked in seamless grace to pleasure her.

And, oh, sweet stars, did he please her. She wrapped her arms tighter around him and clung to him, her body absorbing his rhythm and mirroring it back to him to meet each thrust. She speared her hand through his dark hair and pulled him to her for a kiss, their tongues matching the play of their hips.

The tension that had been building in her threatened to unravel, but he broke the kiss to stare at her with his dark, brooding eyes.

"Not yet." He paused his thrusts, giving her a second to catch her breath, another moment to draw out the pleasure. "Wait for me."

She nodded helplessly, loving the way he could tell her to wait and she would. Maybe it was because she was a strong woman in so many other arenas in life, but she loved giving up power in bed. With someone she trusted.

Her heart caught at the realization of how much she trusted him. Oh, damn. She still loved him so freaking much.

Without words he picked up where he'd left off, his hips making slow, deep thrusts as he gazed into her eyes. Robbed her of reason.

"Now, baby," he crooned, his voice promising wicked delights. "Come with me now."

And like a spellbound follower, she came unraveled in a white-hot flash. Her body pulsed and pulsed inside, her muscles spasming with lush sweetness that radiated bliss to every cell in her body. Romero's taut length seemed to grow within her, pushing her very last boundary until he was one with her.

One heartbeat. One soul.

One overwhelming, undeniable passion.

She shook with the tremors of their release, her body still keyed up and quivering despite the most powerful orgasm of her life. But even as the afterglow lit her inside and filled her with a sense of well-being, she remembered that this was the point at which she would have normally spoken those three little words that bound them together. Three simple syllables that meant their union went beyond the physical.

She probably shouldn't speak those words now. To keep loving Romero when he hadn't said he wanted her back could be the height of foolishness.

For that matter, maybe the orgasm had been as much about a release of pent-up emotions as it had been about the pinnacle of hot sex. She'd been in a tailspin about this man for months, and now, as they lay together in the middle of the Sonoran Desert, she knew they were lost in more ways than one.

Because no matter how close they were to getting back to the States, she didn't think they were any closer to solving the mess they'd made of their relationship.

12

TALK ABOUT LONG, awkward pauses.

Romero didn't just hear it in the ensuing silence, he felt it clear to his toes. The weight of the deed coupled with a handful of unspoken words suddenly anchored him to the earth after soaring so high just moments ago.

It was kind of like the quiet hush of an audience when he finished singing a new song, and he wasn't sure if they were going to cheer or boo him offstage. Only now, as the silence spun out in the chilling air between them, Romero guessed the call for an encore wasn't bloody well coming.

Just as he was wondering what words would soothe over the old wounds and help them to forget about the whole mess of their thwarted relationship, Shannon giggled.

Twitching with quiet laughter, she squirmed beneath him, twisting to one side.

What the—

Then he felt the soft brush of fur against his leg and realized they had company. Shifting to his side, he saw the two coyote pups had followed them into the dense growth and now stood near their feet. One shoved his nose against Shannon's insole, while the darker animal wagged his tail and watched them, as if waiting for approval.

"Aren't they precious?" Shannon scooted away from Romero to pull on her clothes, her gaze locked on the wild dogs.

The tenderness in her eyes damn near flattened him, her expression shifting from the wary defensiveness he'd seen there after sex. In a flash he envisioned her as a mother directing that same tenderness toward her child. The image stole his breath.

Possibly it stole his sanity, too, because he'd never shared his large family's dreams of rampant procreation.

"Don't."

He didn't realize he'd practically shouted that one clipped word until the reverberation bounced back at him.

Shannon stared at him as she tugged her long hair out from under the Ramones T-shirt—his T-shirt—she'd put on. With her other hand, she waggled her fingers to invite the pups close.

"What?" She was already allowing them to sniff her fingers.

"We can't take them with us." He figured it was a lost cause, but, damn it, how could he trek one more mile alongside Shannon with the vision of that maternal glow in his head?

He'd wanted more time with her, another opportunity to see if they could fix what went wrong. But right now, he wasn't sure where to run.

"We're not." She shrugged, oblivious to the sudden drama playing out in his mind. "They're following us." Frowning, she tilted her head to one side and stared up at him, not unlike the pup. "What's the matter with you, anyway? You look like you've seen a ghost."

Ah, man. He was as freaking transparent as a rookie guitar player filling in for a pro.

"I just don't want to see you cornered by a pissed-off mama coyote." Turning away from her, he stood to find the rest of his clothes. "Never let it be said I didn't warn you."

He could feel her watching him as surely as he felt the sunburn crawling over his skin, and he regretted his lack of honesty. Hell, where had he gotten with her in the past by glossing over the stuff that scared the crap out of him?

"I'm warned." Stroking the smaller, lighter animal on the head, she seemed just as grateful as Romero to steer the subject away from what had just happened. "And if their mother can't take better care of these little guys out alone in the desert, then maybe *she* needs to watch out for *me*."

The fierceness in her voice reminded him of how she'd been robbed in the motherhood department herself—both before and after her mom died—and he felt even worse for being scared off by her maternal instincts. Of course she would want to be a great parent.

"I don't think you'll be doing them any favors taking them out of their natural environment." He sounded like a cranky old man.

"Some of us can reach maturity under the strangest of circumstances and still turn out okay." Scooping both dogs into her lap, she buried her face in the fur of the little heads. "I'm not going to ignore them."

"What if they have rabies?"

"They don't look the least bit rabid to me, but if, just if, they are and they nibble my toes, I'll be glad to take the injection when we get back to civilization if it means these guys won't starve out here alone."

"Fine." Romero slumped down beside her on the blanket, acknowledging that he might be overreacting about the whole coyote thing. "But you know they'll never let you bring them over the border, right?" He figured that would at least discourage her.

"So I'll set them down and then whistle for them on the other side. They don't need passports." She didn't even look up as she scratched the white-and-gray ball of fluff behind one ear. "If that mountain lion got their mother, they'll need someone to take care of them."

He didn't bother arguing. Hell, if he wouldn't put up a fight about her moving to New York or not taking a movie role she'd been born to play, why would he bother debating the merits of adopting a couple of wild dogs?

"I'm sorry I kept the condoms a secret." She looked up at him finally, her gaze frank and assessing. "I missed you."

Her simple statement meant more to him than any impassioned declaration, since it had the ring of basic, unvarnished truth.

"That means a lot, since I wouldn't have guessed you thought twice about me after you boxed up all my stuff." He wasn't used to Shannon being so straightforward about how she felt. Usually, her outpourings of emotion were showier—like the time she'd FedExed him twelve pounds of pink candy hearts on the road last Valentine's Day. They'd been custom-designed with "Love ya" and "Studly" written in red.

"No? Have you even been present in this relationship

for the past year, let alone the past twenty hours?" She stopped scratching the pup and he yapped at her in an obvious plea for more.

Hell, even the coyote that'd been chomping on Romero's pants gave up and went over to Shannon.

She shook her head when he didn't respond.

"You should have known I would miss you, because I was the one fighting for us. Remember? It was always worth it to me to try to make things right between us, even if that rocked the boat. It wasn't worth it to you."

"I don't know how you've managed to confuse fighting *with* me to fighting *for* me. But raised voices and demands aren't my idea of—"

"What demands have I ever made of you? That you occasionally remember my existence? Damn it, Romero, ever since you started working on new material, you completely checked out on our relationship. You didn't want to travel, didn't invite me when you met up with guys who played in your band. You are so involved in your own world that even 'I made dinner reservations for us' sounds like a demand to you." Abruptly she stood, kicking up dust and leaving two furry friends in her wake. She reached for her bag as if to take up their hike again, and Romero knew he might not have many other chances with her.

Apparently she'd been giving him more than he'd realized for a while now and he'd been too busy hiding behind his work to notice. Maybe it was past time to come clean—with her *and* with himself.

"I promised myself I'd never get married again."

JUST WHEN SHE THOUGHT she'd heard it all.

Shannon took a moment to let this not-so-stunning revelation sink in. Not because it came as any real surprise—far from it. But because Romero must have a reason for opening this particular can of worms. Here. Now.

Her vintage luggage swung to the ground again, her feet seeming to sink into the sand even though she knew it was an illusion.

"Why?" she asked calmly, since she refused to fight with him. She was done fighting—for him, against him or in any other fashion.

"You've seen my family. The quick-tempered older brothers. The opinionated sisters." He leaned back on the blanket, propping himself up on one elbow. "You know what awaits me if I get married again and have kids."

"Hmm. Unconditional love? A house in the 'burbs? The American dream? Sounds like hell." She almost leaned back against a cactus and got promptly stabbed in the butt. "No wonder you dread it so much."

"Unconditional love? My father didn't speak to me for six years after I walked away from the family business. And even now that he does converse with me, he's still a man of such few words that if I blink, I'll miss it. Do you know my parents have six kids and nineteen grandkids, and every single one of them from the three-year-olds on up thinks they have the answers to all of life's problems, and that they understand everything better than anyone else? My family is like the cult you're lucky to escape—the kind that uses talk torture to brainwash you into submission."

"You're serious." She rubbed a palm over her tush where the cactus needle had stabbed her, then plunked herself down on the ground beside him.

She knew he avoided family gatherings, but he'd

never said anything outright negative about the Jinks clan. He'd felt compelled to bring Shannon to Easter dinner with them the previous year, and she'd been charmed by the noisy, down-to-earth people that had filled the Midwestern farmhouse. Romero had pleaded a work engagement to get out of the festivities early, but Shannon thought that had been because he was stressed and cranky—not that he had deeper issues with them.

"Dead serious." He rubbed his hand over his eyes as if willing away a headache. "I have nothing in common with any of them. Their whole lives revolve around kids and business. Creativity is a waste of time to them—something they were sure to tell me every time I touched a guitar. I couldn't wait to break free of that house."

"And you think that getting married will somehow transform you into a noncreative, argumentative type? Or a cult member?" She shook her head. "I'm not following what the family dynamics have to do with turning you into a commitment-phobe."

Although it wasn't for lack of effort. She was trying her best to fit the pieces together, but was coming up short.

"I caved to their pressure to settle down once. And in the process, I ended up being damn unfair to my ex-wife. She deserved better." Romero shook his head, oblivious to the coyote pups teething on the soles of his boots. "The way I see it, I can have my creativity and a career or I can have a family. I can't see how to have both when one drains all the juice out of the other."

She let that sink in for a moment, weighing her response.

"That's the sorriest excuse for commitment phobia

I've ever heard." She shooed away the dogs from Romero's feet before they tore up the toes of his favorite motorcycle boots. "A couple should bring out the best in each other. Help one another to shine."

She was careful to phrase her response in the third person and not jump into the shoes of the wife in this hypothetical scenario, since she'd been downgraded out of his life. But to be honest, she couldn't help but picture herself in the role as they spoke. She would always put Romero before his family. What wife wouldn't? Besides, he'd always said she was his muse. Couldn't he see that she'd helped his creativity more than she'd stifled it?

"You don't know how overwhelming the pressure can be over time. A person can get lost in it."

She wondered if he even remembered that he'd been with *her* longer than he'd been married. Did he feel that overwhelmed even now? Deciding not to touch that particular explosive topic, she steered the subject away from marriage.

"And as for your family, I thought they were charming." She'd had a great time with his mom and sisters, and hadn't wanted to leave.

"My point exactly. They want to win you over so by the time the wedding rolls around, you'll be convinced that marriage and family are the only way to go."

"We weren't even engaged."

"But we had bought the house together, so they probably thought…"

"We meant something to each other." She brushed some sand from her jeans and willed away the ache in her heart from their breakup.

"Shan—"

She placed a finger over his lips to quiet him. His

voice was too tender and her heart was too raw for her to handle a conversation about their relationship.

"It's okay." Swallowing down a lump in her throat, she snapped her fingers to call over the pups to distract her from the sudden deluge of emotions. "It's not my business anyway, since we aren't together anymore, but you might want to ask yourself if those are your real reasons for avoiding marriage, because they sound just a little..."

"Paranoid?"

"More like self-created drama. Face it, you're letting your family have an awful lot of say in your life." No sooner had she spoken the words than she wondered if she was being a total hypocrite.

Granted, her dysfunctional relationship with her mom appeared on the opposite end of the scale, but hadn't she allowed her mother's lack of interest to mold her into the person she'd become? An entertainer to the core, determined to keep people's attention? With a strong commitment to professionalism, of course, which had been instilled in her by her mom's complete lack of it.

Yeah. Shannon needed to zip her lips on this whole topic, since she had no room to talk.

"Did I mention my last wife lives there? She was an exotic dancer in Vegas until she met my folks. Now she's opening up a wedding-dress shop in the town where I was raised." He crossed his heart. "I swear I'm not making that up."

The situation called for taking the high ground and not commenting. Except that "no comment" went against everything Shannon believed in. Especially since this conversation was the closest Romero had ever come to delving into his issues.

"So now you're convinced that any time your mom and dad get their hands on a girlfriend, she'll morph from a hot chick into a ball and chain." Is this what he thought would happen to *her?* "Romero, maybe your ex jumped into a quickie marriage because she'd never had a family. Some people actually tie the knot to feel the kind of bond you want to escape. But that doesn't mean every woman is looking for that in a relationship."

Were they actually having a conversation about a future together, even though they were dancing around the issue by using hypothetical scenarios? Sure, Shannon had always hoped for a better relationship than her mother had forged with any of the men she'd dated. Like the unnamed man who'd fathered Shannon and hadn't bothered to stick around. But she'd never really looked at her relationship with Romero in that light, always knowing in the back of her mind that he had a reputation for serial monogamy.

At the moment, Shannon couldn't help but wonder if that had been part of the reason she'd felt comfortable with him, knowing their relationship would have a deadline attached. And, God, what did that say about her?

"You're oversimplifying."

"Am I?" Part of her suspected she'd been oversimplifying a lot of things when it came to relationships, since they were a messy, complicated business. Like her feelings for her mother.

"Yes. That would be like me saying you won't take the role playing your mom because you're afraid of finding out she was a hell of a lot tougher in her own way than you give her credit for."

Maybe because Shannon had never been successful in engaging Romero in a fight, she hadn't known that he could deliver a swipe that cut so cleanly you didn't know you were hit for a long moment. Now, she felt the shock of it as she reeled with the blow.

"I know that's only part of it—" he began.

"Point taken." For once, she didn't want to argue, either. She'd had enough epiphanies for one day, thank you very much. Time to retreat to separate corners. "Apparently we've both got a few issues to work through."

Of course, she hadn't realized she had this particular one until ten seconds ago. But the zinger about not wanting to give her mother credit had a ring of truth at its core. No matter that she didn't command the high visibility roles Bridget Leigh had, Shannon could always take pride in the fact that she hadn't had to expose herself. And while everyone would agree Bridget had taken that idea too far, maybe Shannon hadn't taken it far enough. How could she be a strong actress if she didn't expose *something?* Her heart or soul if not her body.

Holy crap, she'd been missing the boat as a performer.

"That was a really shit thing for me to say, wasn't it?"

Romero's palm settled on her leg, gentle and warm. Tentative and strong at the same time.

She peered up at him, surprised to see the worry in his eyes.

"It was a really wise thing to say," she assured him, covering his hand with hers. "You just… What you said surprised me."

"I don't have any right to judge your relationship with your mom. Or anyone else for that matter." His silky voice was heartfelt, a tone that earned him millions more every time he cut a new CD.

She felt damn fortunate to hear it in person.

"No. You have every right, because you know me better than…probably anyone who's ever been in my life." She couldn't stop the flood of tenderness inside her, the rush of affection for a man she'd probably never stopped loving.

Mighty dangerous feelings given how he felt about her and the idea of marriage. But wasn't that the whole problem with her acting? She'd played it too safe in her career, not taking the risks that might have added up to a more substantial résumé. She wouldn't play it safe in her personal life, too.

At least, not anymore.

"Yeah?" He lifted a skeptical eyebrow so high it touched a lock of dark hair spilling onto his forehead. "I'm no Dr. Phil, Shan. What do I know about your family?"

"You know a lot about people and emotions or you wouldn't be able to write songs the whole freaking world relates to."

For that matter, Romero might not put himself on the line in their relationship, but he sure as heck put himself out there in his music. Maybe he didn't have much left for their fights because it all went into lyrics. Which, while it wasn't ideal, reassured her that Romero might harbor strong feelings about her, after all. She had been trying to avoid hearing his songs on the radio for months after their breakup, fearing they would tear her heart out. But maybe if she listened to more of this quiet man's music, she'd gain a little more access to his soul.

In fact, that kind of channeling was what she needed to do for her work. Instead of always baring her heart to Romero, spilling all of her emotions into a relationship that he didn't want anymore, she should put more of that into her performances.

Her heart seemed to break wide-open with understanding. Love and gratitude flowed from her, no matter how broken her relationship with Romero had become. As soon as they got back home, she planned to start funneling these insights into her work. Her art. That movie about Bridget Leigh, if the offer was still on the table.

But for right now, the only outlet for the sudden rush of emotions sat beside her, his brown eyes hooded and thoughtful.

"Romero?"

She scoped out the space around them and noticed the coyote pups were sleeping in a ball together nearby, their heads pillowed on each other's bellies. The sun's rays were cut by the dense growth of monster-size cacti, shading them at the harshest time of day. All the rest of the world was quiet.

"What?" He took out a water bottle and tipped it back for a long swig before he passed it to her.

"I know that you're in charge of the condom stash." She reached to trail her fingers over his shirt pocket where he'd stuffed the remaining two foil packets. "But what if I told you I'd make it worth your while to send this relationship out on a high note?"

13

HEAD STILL spinning from a conversation that had dredged up a lot of the brokenness in their past, Romero couldn't believe Shannon wanted…what she seemed to want.

Yet here she was, walking her fingertips up his chest in an unmistakable message.

God help him, he'd never understand women. Shannon in particular. But he wouldn't let an opportunity to touch her again slide from his grasp. Not when she'd apologized for packing up his things. Not when she might leave L.A. for New York, where he'd never see her again.

If nothing else, he planned to leave her with memories to rock her world. A belated Valentine's gift.

"You want to go out on a high note?" He smoothed a strand of her hair between his thumb and forefinger, savoring the silky texture. "It just so happens I'm an expert in notes. High ones. Low ones. Complex chords."

He dipped his head to kiss the side of her neck. The scents of her shampoo and sunscreen mingled there and he inhaled deeply. She shivered, the soft tremor evident beneath his lips where they grazed her skin.

"I still think I could teach you a thing or two." She

splayed a hand on his chest, covering the place where his heart thumped out its own brand of mating call.

Damn, but he wanted her.

Already. Again.

"I lived the rock 'n' roll lifestyle for a lot of years, baby girl." In reality, he hadn't been one of those guys who picked up women just because they were available; his taste was too discerning to be satisfied with just anyone. But he knew Shannon liked to bust his chops about it, and he had fun indulging this woman. "What makes you think you can teach me anything new?"

One eyebrow arched in an expression her bombshell mom had made famous. He wondered if Shannon had any idea how similar she looked to Bridget Leigh right now.

Similar, but hotter. Sexier. His.

If only for a little while.

"You forget who you're dealing with." She traced a light circle on his chest with one hand while her other reached for the snap on her jeans. "I guess I'll have to remind you."

After a flick of her wrist and a graceful rise to her feet, she shimmied out of her jeans. The denim caught once or twice, but with a roll of her hips, she freed herself from the confining cloth. The sight of her bare legs shouldn't have been anything new to him. But she didn't just drop her clothes.

Like any good entertainer, she worked it.

Thumbs dipped into the waistband of her panties and she tugged the elastic down just a little, as if the pink satin were a holster. She swaggered and pranced to an invisible tune, teasing him with what she hadn't yet unveiled.

Blowing him kisses, she turned her back to him and

danced her body low to the ground, peering over her shoulder all the while to gauge his expression. Or, hell, with the way her eyes went to his crotch, maybe that wasn't what she was gauging at all.

Heat blasted through his veins, firing a need that was incredibly primal given how many times they'd been together. How many times they'd seduced each other.

"I might not be able to wait long enough for you to teach me anything."

"But you haven't watched me on-screen in months. I thought I'd put on a good show for you today to make up for it." She wrapped her arms around her waist and gyrated with slow, deliberate movements. "I thought you might like to see me onstage for a private performance."

Grabbing the hem of her shirt, she inched it up, up. Then, turning toward him, she rubbed the cotton over her breasts, clearly enjoying the friction for a long moment before she pulled the shirt the rest of the way off.

Exposing her breasts in the pink satin-and-lace bra.

He wanted nothing more than to surge to his feet and drag her down to the ground so he could have her underneath him. But she seemed to have something else in mind, and, damn it, if she got off on long, slow sexual teasing, he could handle it. Couldn't he?

At least for a few seconds more.

"You'd feel better if I was touching you right now." He dug his fingers into his thighs to keep from reaching for her.

"But sometimes I just want to be your undivided center of attention." She slipped a finger under one of her bra straps and flicked it off her shoulder. Her necklace glittered against her skin as it caught a shaft of sunlight. "I like the feel of your eyes on me."

He knew he hadn't always provided that for her—a rapt audience. And at that moment he understood she planned to change that in the future, although maybe not with him. Something in her eyes told him she would never settle for less than commanding one-hundred-percent attention again.

Regret that he hadn't given that to her burned as hot as his body's need to have her.

"Well, I'm giving you a standing ovation here, I guaran-damn-tee you that." His rock-hard response to her show was a zipper buster.

"That's where the second act comes in." She dropped to her knees and crawled a couple of paces, her shoulder blades rising and falling like a predator cat as she made her way toward him.

The view of her cleavage was spectacular, her rosy, dark nipples barely visible through a swath of pink lace at the top of her bra. With each slither closer to him, her breasts bounced and swayed, threatening to spill right out of the lingerie.

He thought he'd spontaneously combust as she lowered her cheek to his thigh and stroked her face against him, her warm breath seeping into his clothes and firing his need to be naked.

"We're only at the second act?" He gulped. Tried not to swallow his own tongue.

"You'll like this one." She lifted her head and planted a kiss on his abs, just above the waist of his jeans. "Honest."

His breath rasped through his lungs so hard he wasn't

sure he could hear her anymore. Her lips moved, but his brain requisitioned all its gray matter to envision her mouth…somewhere else.

Then she yanked open his snap with her teeth and he started praying for restraint. In fact, while her pearly whites yanked down his zipper with slow precision, he ground his molars into oblivion trying to hold back.

Trying not to rip her remaining clothes off and pump into her with animalistic fervor.

Having successfully unfastened his jeans, she tugged them off him now. He watched her narrow back as she worked, her spine moving sinuously while she maneuvered her satin-clad hips.

Pausing to peer up at him, she licked her lips and he nearly lost his mind.

With a growl, he reached for her, but she ducked under his arms to kiss his shaft. Her soft mouth molded to him through the cotton of his boxers.

"Shan." It took a hell of a lot of concentration to form words. "This, uh, second act has a lot of tension."

Nudging his boxers down with one finger, she landed a real kiss on the tip of his cock, her tongue darting out to encircle him.

"You like the rising action?" she asked, her hips twitching back and forth hypnotically while she licked a path from tip to base of him.

He went dizzy with the feel of it, his eyes crossing and his head swimming with visions of what he wanted to do to her.

"A little too well."

Unable to withstand another second of her one-woman show, he hauled her up in his arms and rolled her to her back. Air whooshed in and out of his lungs like a racehorse in the final stretch.

Shannon's eyes fixed on him, her pupils so wide there was only the smallest ring of deep blue around the edges. Her lips were swollen and red from kissing him, her hair tousled from her performance.

"And you think *I'm* guilty of too much enthusiasm in this relationship?" Her satisfied smile told him she wasn't minding his, er—passionate nature.

Still, he found himself wanting to turn that smile into an expression of total bliss.

"I save my enthusiasm for the moments that are most deserving." He dipped his head to kiss his way down her neck.

Shannon closed her eyes to savor the feel of Romero's mouth on her, the stubble from his cheek gently abrading her skin while his tongue stirred a longing deep within her. She gave herself over to him completely, to experience the keen pleasure of being loved by this man. She would enjoy this time no matter what the outcome, savor every second of lush indulgence a woman felt when wrapped in the arms of a man who knew how to pleasure her.

His hard body imprinted itself on her softness, molding her breasts and pressing for entrance between her thighs. His flesh heated hers, sparking a flash fire across her skin. She loved the weight of him pinning her down—not too heavy, but substantial enough to make her feel deliciously in his command.

When his mouth reached her breast, she squirmed with a hunger she couldn't ignore. Arching her back, she rubbed herself shamelessly against him. Sweet sensation radiated through her whole body, concentrating into a sharp ache between her legs. She clamped her thighs around his erection, savoring the hot length of him. Maybe she could tease him until he saw reason. Until he pushed his way inside her.

Reaching between them, she drew a circle around the tip of his cock with one finger, smoothing the dampness across the blunt head of him until he growled low in his throat. Her sensual maneuvering worked every bit as well as she could have hoped, for he slid inside her in one long stroke, burying himself deep.

Her breath halted; her whole body froze for one endless moment of perfect completion. She couldn't remember another instance where sex had felt so sublime, a time when bells seemed to peal and angels shouted out giddy alleluias.

She wrenched her eyes open, wanting to see if Romero was experiencing the same sensory high as her. He stared back, his gaze fixed on hers. Except that, instead of the rapturous expression she expected, he appeared stunned. Surprised.

Maybe that was rapture for him.

Unwilling to lose a second of this incredible feeling, Shannon locked her legs around his waist and hitched her ankles together as her eyes slid closed again. She held him there and lifted her hips, needing everything he had to give.

"Shannon—"

She blocked out any words that might take away from the sensation building between her thighs. She dug her fingers into his muscular shoulders and inhaled the musky scent of his skin and then—

Her orgasm hit her like a freight train—sudden, surprising and powerful. Tremors rumbled through her with seductive force, squeezing her whole body tight.

She was so caught up in the delicious release that it took her a second to realize Romero was pulling out of her. Untwining her legs, wrenching his hips back, away from hers.

Confused and still shuddering from reaching that physical pinnacle, Shannon couldn't comprehend what was happening. Romero levered himself up and off her. He half turned his body, his shoulders shaking with his release while one hand guided his cock away from her.

His seed spilled harmlessly to the side, his erection naked to the world.

He hadn't worn a condom.

And even more distressing, she'd been too caught up in the sex to realize the gargantuan risk they'd just taken.

14

"WHAT JUST HAPPENED?"

Her voice sounded hoarse and Shannon wondered if she was going into shock.

It wasn't that far-fetched. What woman wouldn't have a no-holds-barred freak-out when birth control wasn't used?

"I think we both know what just happened."

Romero's voice didn't sound much steadier than hers. Although in his case, Shannon thought he seemed more irritated than panicked. And wouldn't that be just like a man?

"That's where you're wrong, because I was too caught up in the moment to notice—"

His hard stare halted her words. His raised eyebrow confirmed her dawning suspicion.

"You…" She cleared her throat and tried again. "You were that caught up in the moment, too?"

His curt nod confirmed the obvious.

"I wasn't thinking." He rolled to one side to retrieve his bag and then dug around for a shirt to clean himself off. "I was…I don't know. So focused on making you feel good or so determined to make this something we'd never forget." His laugh was a bark of self-deprecation.

"Guess I might have damn well managed that, didn't I? I'm sorry, Shannon."

The expression on his face was new to her. He'd never been a man to pour out his emotions except in song or maybe sex. So to see him now with a mixture of tenderness and worry in his eyes, she could almost forget her own fears enough to enjoy this uncharacteristic moment.

Almost.

"Do you know what this means?" She felt her breath whoosh in and out of her lungs with alarming speed, even though she didn't seem to be getting nearly enough air. Her head spun. Pressure built behind her eyes.

"We need to find birth control that doesn't require application in the heat of the moment?"

So much for his short-lived sensitivity.

"No." She shook her head and the motion made her so dizzy she reached out to feel solid ground with her hand. "It means I could be pregnant."

THE WORDS WOULD terrorize any self-respecting bachelor.

Logically, Romero knew this. So he had no earthly clue why he hadn't broken out in a cold sweat yet. He pulled Shannon into his arms and held her close, whispering all the right things. That it would be okay. That they would figure this out together. That he would stay with her no matter what happened.

And none of those comforting clichés stuck in his throat. In fact, as he kissed the top of her head and stroked her hair, he realized he meant every single one with a fierceness he would never have expected.

The fierceness of a…family man?

The panic didn't kick in the way he always feared it would. He'd run from the possibility of a family for so long he'd assumed it was an instinct that would always be there. But right now as he looked down at the amazing woman in front of him, the woman who'd been his muse, his sex partner, his roommate and the most fun traveling companion ever, he couldn't scrounge up the old fears.

"Do you mean it?" Shannon pulled away, her gaze latching on to his as he struggled to recall what it was about the family thing that always used to scare the crap out of him.

Oh, yeah. The paralyzing effect on a person's independence and creativity. A few rogue doubts hit him and he swallowed hard.

"Yes." He nodded automatically to reinforce the affirmative. And, damn it, he did mean what he'd said about sticking with her through this. He just didn't want to end up back in Iowa selling car parts.

Well, maybe that was stretching things given his current bank balance, but the magnitude of what had just happened had him spinning in circles. How could he possibly process it all?

"You're freaking out." Shannon's brows knit together while her lips pursed with worry. And despite a four-year age gap between them, he had the sudden but distinct impression her emotional maturity outpaced his by a few decades at least.

He knew this was a hell of time to finally "encounter his feelings" the way Shannon had been asking him to for a year. But he couldn't seem to do one damn thing about it. Long-suppressed fears practically erupted inside him.

"I'm fine." A fine freaking mess. "It's just—this is a lot to think about for both of us."

He willed a calming tone into his voice even though the ground had just fallen out from under his feet. And what a crap time to deal with this, when they needed all their focus and energy to get out of the desert in one piece.

With a jerky nod, she extricated herself from his arms and pushed herself to her feet.

"Would you excuse me for a minute?" Scooping up her clothes, she pulled on a T-shirt and her jeans. "I just need a little air."

The coyote pups reappeared from wherever they'd been playing, their tails already wagging.

"Are you okay?" Romero had no idea what his role should be at this point. Those few moments of being sure he was saying the right thing had evaporated when his brain got a better handle on what this all meant.

He needed some air himself.

"I'm fine." She tried to smile, failed miserably and ended up nodding vigorously. "Fine."

And, practically tripping over her sore feet, she lit out of the cactus forest and back into the open desert, the pups at her heel.

Romero dug out a bottle of water, wishing like hell it was bourbon, and took a long drink. Then another. He needed to get his head on straight before Shannon came back.

He didn't know what scared him more. The fact that the initial image of Shannon pregnant hadn't freaked him out. Or the fact that translating that event into a big-picture view of his life—and what it meant for his relationship with his siblings and parents—had made him come unglued. Either way, he knew he couldn't allow his family phobias to hurt Shannon. Whether or not they reconciled their differences, she deserved his support until they were sure she wasn't…expecting.

And after that?

One of the coyote pups returned just then, the lighter-colored one with an ear that liked to flop forward.

"Hey, fur ball." Romero held his hand out for the dog to sniff, grateful for nonhuman company that wouldn't give a rip if he said the wrong thing. "Did you come back for a little more quiet time?"

He pictured Shannon jogging laps around the desert or maybe indulging in a few kickboxing moves to let off some steam after what had just happened. She was high energy, no doubt about it.

The dog wagged its tail as if agreeing.

"But for all her crazy hours and her last-minute parties that fill the whole damn house all weekend long, she definitely keeps things interesting." He'd never had the kind of life Shannon had brought his way, a homey existence so different from the bleak sameness of the days of his childhood, where the focus had been on constant hard work without taking time to celebrate much of anything.

As he scratched the pup's soft neck, Romero realized that life without Shannon would be as empty and colorless as a rock 'n' roll arena the day after a gig.

"I never really thought I'd find someone to make family life seem fun." He'd been raised to think of it as a constant obligation, a responsibility to put first. But no one had ever made it sound like something…

exciting. "And Shannon is definitely that. But life with her is also a full-color drama, complete with a live audience and round-the-clock public interest."

And he hated living under the microscope. Their breakup fight had been chronicled in papers and tabloid TV across the country. When he thought about trying to make another go of it with Shannon, he had to wonder if he'd be overcorrecting the downside of his own childhood, substituting a nonstop spotlight for the dreary boredom of eking out a living with nothing to discuss except the weather and the state of the economy.

"Arf!" The little pup wagged its tail, and Romero couldn't help but think the dog was taking Shannon's side.

Downing the last of his water, Romero hoped the liquid would wash away the lingering unrest pinging around his insides at the idea of fatherhood and family. He would resent life under the microscope even more if there was a kid in the picture. But maybe part of that was because he'd had his time in the spotlight. Knew enough about fame to understand it wasn't all it was cracked up to be.

Didn't Shannon deserve the chance to experience the limelight at its brightest, too? Sure, she'd been followed around all her life because of her famous parent, but she'd never had a chance to know the attention was all about her—her talents and her ability to breathe life into characters.

She deserved the chance to discover how incredible she could really be on-screen. And if a baby delayed her dreams, would she resent him for not having kept his wits during sex?

He allowed himself to envision her as a mother, a role

she would play more beautifully than any other. The image in his head—of her cradling his child to her breast and glowing with that radiant Shannon sweetness—socked the breath right out of his lungs. He couldn't walk away from that, even if she guilted him into building a house down the street from his close-knit clan who resented anyone who tried to make it out of the Midwest.

Even if his father never forgave him for leaving home, Orson Jinks would welcome a grandchild from his youngest son. Romero knew it without question. He would bore the new addition with a bunch of sappy tales of his chore-burdened childhood that had supposedly built character. Lots of kids without a stable home life would have envied Romero the father he had, but he couldn't help it that he'd always longed for broader horizons.

"You're right," he told the coyote, holding his hand above the pup's head to encourage him to jump. "Shannon deserves better than what I've given her, pregnant or not."

He had his head screwed on straight. For her, he'd find a way to deal with his family that didn't involve a ten-state barrier at all times. For Shannon, he could try to carve out a life as a family man, even if the idea still gave him the occasional round of hives as he remembered the dinner table shouting matches, with everyone convinced they knew best and had a right to weigh in on one another's problems.

But he wouldn't let her give up her dreams for the sake of family, the way his father guilted almost everyone around him into doing. Because while Romero knew that his dramatic, emotional lover would pour herself into her new role with enthusiasm, he didn't want his child to be the reason she walked away from her career.

At least, he hoped that Shannon's happiness was his real motive and not those ghosts of his "family before all else" past.

15

SHE MIGHT NOT BE Hollywood's reigning queen, but Shannon knew enough about acting to recognize the abject fear in Romero's eyes at the thought of having a baby. And his rookie attempts to hide the worries under a tight smile and reassuring words.

If he wasn't such a gentleman, he would be sprinting back to the California state line right now. For that matter, if he hadn't been such a gentleman and offered her a ride in the first place, he would have surely been far better off. He had more endurance than she did, and this wasn't the first time he'd struck out into the wild on his own. From broken-down tour buses that left him in the middle of nowhere to his weekend fishing expeditions, Romero Jinks knew how to fend for himself. It was only when he had a diva in high heels teetering at his side that he couldn't make good headway.

Collapsing on the sand a few hundred yards from the thicket of dense cacti where they'd made love, Shannon allowed life to steamroll her. The pregnancy panic wouldn't scare her so much if she didn't know full well that Romero had big-time trouble committing. A fact she'd grasped from the day she'd moved in to play house with him. A fact she'd tried to forget no matter how often he'd reinforced the walls between their worlds even while under the same roof.

He'd made a few vague allusions to a tempestuous upbringing and a controlling father who resented Romero—or any of the kids—striking off on his or her own. But was that really enough to explain away Romero's commitment phobia? Surely he understood every family was different, that he didn't need to raise his children the same way his dad did.

Romero's need for a footloose lifestyle seemed to go beyond that. He and Shannon had spent most of the past year working in different cities, often on different continents. He hadn't met her in the cities where he played, but kept their rendezvous on the down low at a neutral location. Even when they were both in residence in Hollywood, he'd retreated to his studio, keeping night-owl hours to write while she slept.

All of her attempts to draw him into a real relationship—to work through their problems—had met with silence or retreat every time. Right up until the grand finale when his tire tracks had left their mark on the driveway.

Of course he wasn't going to suddenly morph into Joe Family Man.

The darker-haired puppy licked her cheek, the soft rub of warm tongue making her realize he was swiping at her tears. Damn it.

"I'm not crying over him," she assured the coyote, pulling him onto her lap to snuggle close while wondering where the lighter-haired pup had gone. "I'm just crying over my own cluelessness for getting wrapped up with a man who..."

She couldn't finish the thought, since her heart wouldn't let her lie about what she felt for him. How could she write off Romero's flaws with snarky summations when she had as many and maybe more?

"Okay, maybe I'm crying over him a little. But he *has* been voted Sexiest Man Alive. And he writes beautiful music." One of the reasons she'd fallen for him was his brooding, moody songs, which spoke to her soul.

It only stood to reason that a man who wrote music like that would have a similar emotional side. So she totally should have known what she was getting into when she signed on to be with him. How could she blame him now for retreating from arguments? For all she knew, the brooding helped him write. She'd never even asked, preferring to think anyone who didn't express feelings the same way she did had to have it wrong.

"Maybe I didn't handle the whole thing very well when we broke up," she confided to the coyote, lowering her nose to nuzzle soft puppy fur. "I pushed him away by demanding he argue with me. Maybe he thinks that having kids with me means bringing children into a noisy or—hell—confrontational household."

Just saying the words aloud rocked her world. With her mother's poor example, Shannon would make sure she read every parenting book in print to get her tactics down before having a kid. Didn't Romero know that? The idea that he didn't came like a lightning flash to her baby-addled brain.

Then another flash came—this one all too real.

Blinking at the sudden spot of brightness a few yards away, Shannon peered toward the cactus thicket and thought she saw movement. Romero?

Setting the puppy down, she wondered what to say to him next. She hadn't meant to get all emotional back there, but even if she could live with a man who didn't like to show his emotions, she couldn't keep a padlock on hers all the time.

"Romero?" She squinted into the thicket just as another flash almost blinded her.

Like the sun beaming off glass. A small point of glass that looked like—

A camera lens.

"Romero!" She screamed for him as the reflected light in the lens bobbed crazily and then disappeared.

A ruckus sounded within the cactus copse, and she knew whoever had been watching her was beating a hasty retreat.

Romero came barreling out of the thicket a stone's throw north of where the camera had been.

"That way!" she shouted, pointing as she ran toward the spot where she'd seen someone. "A man."

Her rock 'n' roll hero took off like a sprinter at the sound of a shot, his jeans only half buttoned and his feet bare. Shannon ran, too, but she knew she'd never catch up.

"He was pointing a camera at me!" she called, wishing she had her running shoes and feet that weren't trashed from yesterday's trek.

Romero leaped into the cactus clusters with no regard for the sharp spines, and Shannon lost sight of him. Of both of them. But she heard the rustle of bodies and skidded to a stop just outside the towering desert plants.

"Do you see him?" She didn't know if the man could offer a ride home or if he had an operable cell phone, but they needed him.

As for why he'd be pointing his camera lens at her as if she were some kind of wildlife, Shannon had no idea. No one even knew where she was, so it wasn't like the bloodsucking paparazzi would be down here.

"I got him," Romero shouted, his tone as guttural and dark as she'd ever heard it.

And by the strain in his voice, Shannon suspected the man hadn't submitted by choice. Worry gnawed at her. She didn't want to end up in some Mexican prison for detaining a local against his will.

"Uh, Romero?" she called, just as two bodies came charging out of the desert vegetation toward her.

One sweaty, middle-aged bald man sporting drug-store Wayfarers and a surf shop T-shirt, followed by studly, shirtless Romero. Who had his hand wrapped around the other guy's neck.

"What are you doing?" Her voice faded to barely there in a moment of hysteria. She'd never before seen such an angry look gleaming in Romero's eyes.

"Help!" the other man shouted, his cheeks red from the struggle, his arms flailing against the pressure at his neck.

Scared for him and for whatever craziness had taken over Romero, she stalked closer, trying to get into her lover's line of sight.

"Stop." Reaching into the fray, she put her hand on Romero's arm.

"He's a tabloid hound." Romero yanked a camera from around the man's neck and she realized the strap of the device had been what was wrapped around the stranger's throat. "He's got a VW van parked on a dirt trail in there."

A VW van? Crinkling her nose, she tried to recall why that was significant.

"It's the guy who ran us off the road, Shan." Romero kept the camera out of the other man's reach while he turned it on and flipped through the stored files. "He's been following us ever since the wedding. He probably heard me offer to drive you home, and figured he'd capture the reunion story on film."

Dumbfounded, Shannon swung toward the surf shop dude. "You what?" Anger simmered, heating her more than her sunburned skin. "You ran us off the road, subjected us to a mountain lion and nearly killed us for a *photo op?*"

Her gaze connected with his, this slimy man who had pleaded for help just moments ago. How dare he ask for aid when he could have killed them?

"You know how much the papers will pay for a photo of you two back together? I didn't mean to hurt you. I just needed that payday, man."

"Did you know we've been lost in the desert ever since?" She watched the man's jaw thrust out in defiance. "We could have died in that crash, trying to avoid you. Did you know the roof caved halfway in? That we *flipped over?*"

The dude's chest deflated at the chiding, the colorful surfboards printed on his shirt blurring into a muted swirl as his shoulders slumped.

"I think he had a pretty good idea we were lost, judging by the footage." Romero held the camera out to her so she could see something on the view screen.

An image of her showering naked under the stars. The picture was so crisp and clear he had to have shot it from close range.

The photo-snapping pond scum voyeur leaned over

to see what had caught their attention, and actually had the nerve to smile.

"I used the flash when her eyes were closed." He pointed a hairy finger at the screen. "I needed more light in this back corner, but considering the equipment I had, I thought it turned out incredibly well." He angled his head to glance at Romero. "I can make you copies."

"You smug bastard." She launched herself at the sweaty man, incensed by his lack of remorse.

"Hey." Romero inserted himself between them, imprisoning her arms in a powerful grip. "Let's just focus on getting home, and then deal with all this once we cross the border, okay?"

It took her a moment for the words to settle in her overwrought brain.

"Home?" The notion sounded so far from reality she almost couldn't believe they could go back now.

"Yeah, this guy's got a van and I'm sure the least he can do for nearly killing us is give us a lift back to L.A." The threatening scowl Romero sent to Sweaty Neck hit its mark and the guy nodded.

"Absolutely. Sure. I'm ready to head back whenever you are." He stepped away from Shannon, though, wisely keeping his distance.

"I'm not riding in the same vehicle as this man."

"Steve Selby." He fumbled in his pants pocket and withdrew a card. "Selby Photos."

The coyote pups at Shannon's feet barked at the man until he dropped his business card back in his pocket.

"Look." Romero put his arm around her and turned them both away from Steve. "We need to get home and this guy's van is our fastest option. Besides, we want to make sure he hasn't already downloaded those photos somewhere."

Her shoulders went rigid. "You think they could already be circulating?" Memories of how hard she'd fought not to cash in on her sexpot heritage made her stomach clench.

Had she worked so long not to appear a carbon copy of her mother, only to have this man sabotage those efforts in a heartbeat, with underhanded tactics?

"I hope not, but we'll bring charges for the accident if he has. Either way, I think we need to talk to him." Romero's calm voice of reason made sense although she'd much prefer to simply smash the man's stupid camera to smithereens and leave him to fend for himself in the desert the way she'd had to.

Then again, she'd had Romero with her. She hated to think what would have happened to her during the past twenty-four hours if she hadn't.

Strange to think how many ways he'd saved her, and now they would be going back to separate lives. He would be out of her life for good once they reached L.A. Because even if they shared the miracle of a baby together, Shannon knew his commitment issues would only allow him to be a wonderful father—not a wonderful significant other. Just the idea of returning to the reality of their messy breakup made her hesitant to climb into the VW van.

"Okay." Nodding stiffly, she agreed, knowing her time with Romero had finally run out.

16

SHANNON'S HEART WAS in the process of breaking as she handed the two coyote pups over to a sympathetic border patrol agent. Her old friend who worked at the crossing wasn't there that day, but mentioning his name had won her a few points—enough to find some help with the animals.

Finally coralling them long enough to establish their gender, she'd named the pups on the long ride north. Mary-Kate was the wild and crazy light-haired dog. Ashley was the darker, more serious of the pair. Shannon adored them both, but the U.S. Customs agents wouldn't hear of letting them into the country. As if the dang dogs couldn't have run across the invisible border on their own at any given time.

"It's okay, sweetie," the freckled, red-haired older border agent assured Shannon as she led her and the pups into a back room inside the patrol station. "My best friend has a shelter on this side of the border that rescues all kinds of animals in these sorts of situations. But these two are so young, they should be able to get right back out in the wild with a little help. Don't you worry about a thing."

Shannon nodded mutely because, while she would miss Mary-Kate and Ashley terribly, she couldn't deny the tears spilling from her eyes had more to do with the impending loss of the man she'd spent almost a year of her life with. A man who might have fathered her child in a heated moment of lovemaking.

A man who wasn't ready to commit, no matter what he said to the contrary.

"Honestly, this woman's facility is huge and she's done a great job with fund-raising, so everything from captured pythons to misplaced llamas find good homes there," the customs agent continued, accompanying Shannon into an area that looked like a break room. She pulled a couple of pieces of cheese from a minifridge. "I'm Rita, by the way."

Shannon grasped the agent's offered hand and squeezed, grateful that someone had taken pity on her plea to help the animals.

"I'm Shannon—"

"Shannon Leigh." Rita grinned as she shook Shannon's hand. "We all recognized you and that handsome rock star you're with."

Shannon's good manners told her to smile and be gracious with this nice lady who was doing her a huge favor. But as Rita leaned down to give Mary-Kate and Ashley some cheese, the dam broke and Shannon's tears started flowing in earnest.

"Oh!" The agent straightened as Shannon tried to muffle a choked sob. "Honey, what's wrong? Is it that bad-boy rock 'n' roll man of yours?" Pulling out a chair from the small plastic table in the break room, she tugged a mortified Shannon into it.

"I'm fine," she protested, even though her world was falling apart like a sitcom during a writers' strike.

"Okay, and I'm Hollywood's It Girl," Rita retorted, lowering herself to sit across from her. "Come on, sweetie, it's just us here and I'm not some blabbermouth to sell you out. For that matter, I'm sure I'd get in trouble with work if I tried to cash in on any of the stories I've seen come across this border, and there've been more than a few. Are you okay?"

Collecting herself, Shannon took the tissue Rita handed her. Romero and Steve Selby were in a holding room speaking to other border agents about what had happened in Mexico.

"I'm just a little unsettled after that stupid photographer ran us off the road and followed us without us knowing." Her skin crawled when she thought about the way he'd taken pictures of her naked. "And Romero and I got close again after the big breakup. But now that the whole ordeal in the desert is over, I know he'd be just as happy to dissolve our relationship once again."

Rita made a tsking noise and moved the whole box of tissues over to the plastic table. "Then I say you ought to show him what it feels like to be split. Honey, I stood up and cheered for that stunt you pulled with the clothes in the driveway. Sometimes we need to stand up for ourselves and what we want. And men— God love them—sometimes they need the strong message or they just don't flipping hear what we're trying to say."

"But he thinks I'm argumentative, and he's probably right, so—"

"So don't argue anymore." Rita whacked the table forcefully, her kind brown eyes going dark and fierce.

"You go your own way and let him go his, and you just let him try that loneliness on for size, you hear?"

Shannon smiled at this total stranger's heartfelt opinion on her life. Being under the Hollywood microscope might stink sometimes, but right now, it felt nice to have this woman understand where she was coming from and what she'd been dealing with.

"You're right." Blowing her nose one last time, she vowed she wouldn't go begging Romero to stick around when he didn't want to. Moreover, she wouldn't take him up on his offer to stay with her just because of the slim chance a sperm and egg did the happy dance this weekend. "I will be the cool, composed female in the face of big drama."

Sort of like her screen characters, right? She'd leverage her real emotions for her performances and utilize some of her reserved cinematic subtlety with the man who couldn't abide theatrics. It was a perfect plan.

And one Romero damn well ought to appreciate, since he'd suggested at least half of that equation himself.

"That's a girl." Rita nodded her approval and rubbed an encouraging hand on Shannon's shoulder. "You can do it."

Swiping away the last of her tears, Shannon sure as hell hoped so.

SHANNON HAD TURNED stone-cold silent by the time she returned to the holding room in the border patrol station.

Romero chalked up some of that quiet to her parting with the coyote pups, since even her famous face hadn't helped her sweet-talk the hard-asses at the border. Fortunately, the two pups had attracted plenty of attention around the customs complex and a particularly pet-crazy agent had convinced Shannon to let her take them to a friend who ran a rescue shelter.

So as heart tugging as the parting with the pups had been, Romero didn't think that accounted for Shannon's unusual quiet. Around them, phones rang and computers chimed—typical office noises. Conversations in Spanish and English bounced into the bare room through the door open to the main building.

"You want me to sue him?" he asked as they waited with the slimeball photographer in a holding area for people without proper identification.

They had identification, but because he'd been driving another guy's van and had filed a claim about his crashed vehicle, all three of them had needed to give statements about what had happened in Mexico.

Romero had meant to cheer Shannon out of her quiet mood, but Selby piped up.

"You people can't expect privacy when you build your careers with the help of our hard work." The sleazy cameraman jabbed a thumb at his own chest, asserting a kind of power that only existed in his head. "There's legal precedent for my right to follow you."

"Tell that to Princess Di," Shannon retorted, her eyes flicking over him with derision.

The smarmy scum was beginning to tick Romero off all over again. In the name of getting back on U.S. soil, he'd temporarily set aside his fury at this jerk for filming Shannon in the buff, not to mention endangering her life. But his anger was on a short leash.

"Not when the photographer purposely stranded the celebrity and did them bodily harm in the process." He ground his teeth as he remembered the god-awful fear when he'd seen Shannon's head bleeding after the accident.

Selby shut up.

"That's okay," Shannon said finally, swiping her hair behind her shoulder, the picture of cool, calm and collected. "I'm content as long as we have the camera and we reserve the right to file charges if the photos show up anywhere."

She shot Selby a level look, reminding Romero how tough she could be. Despite the diva exterior and the overbred dogs she liked to dress in matching outfits, Shannon was as savvy a Tinseltown businesswoman as he'd ever met. She protected her image and her career with a fierceness he wished he'd had in his early days in the limelight.

"Sounds like a plan." He wanted to take her out of the holding room, to talk to her in private, since they'd left the desert with a whole new set of issues between them. But he didn't know the protocol here and the border patrol folks, while nice enough, seemed fairly hard-core about their job.

No way would he risk pissing them off and getting sent back to Mexico tonight.

Still, if there was any way to have a word with her alone—

"Ms. Leigh?" A patrolman stuck his head in the door, a sheaf of paperwork in his hand. "Your agent is here. A Ms. Ceily. You're free to go."

Romero stood, but not before Shannon was on her feet.

"Thank God," she muttered, pulling her dusty satchel onto her shoulder.

His throat dried up at the sight of her back. She wasn't just running away from a problem the way he had lots of times. The way she had done briefly out in the desert when she'd realized their birth control mishap.

This time, she would be leaving for good.

A notion that made all his fear of getting sucked into the doldrums of family life pale in comparison. He didn't want to tie Shannon to him that way—with some kind of guilt-induced sense that they needed to stay together for the sake of a baby—but he also couldn't stomach the thought of not knowing his own kid.

"Shannon." He couldn't resist this chance to put his hand on her waist and gently steer her toward the door. "Can I have a word with you? Alone."

He glanced at the shutterbug still seated at the holding-room table, Romero's eyes communicating the consequences if the jackass tried to listen in on a private conversation.

"Sure." Shannon followed his lead and stepped outside the door before turning to him in the hallway, her eyes distant. Remote. "What's up?"

A couple of agents strode past with a tearful Mexican mama and her toddler daughter between them. The sight of the silent border drama probably played out ten times a day here reminded Romero how small his problems were compared to what other people lived with. No one was stopping him from making a good living or from residing wherever he chose.

He needed to get over himself and find a way to tell Shannon he'd be there for her, even if a full-blown family wasn't the type of future he'd mapped out for himself.

"I want you to stay at the house until we can figure this out." He said the first thing that came to mind, since he hadn't planned this spiel and had zero practice in making a commitment any more serious than what he'd already shared with her.

"I'm not staying." Shaking her head, she dismissed the idea out of hand. "I have to meet with the producers in New York next week no matter what I decide about *Baby Doll*. But thank you."

He didn't physically take a step back, but in his head, he was reeling from that revelation.

"You're leaving? Already?"

Frowning, she shrugged. "I can't afford not to work, what with the kind of mortgage we've got."

"Geez, Shan. I'm not some kind of evil landlord who's going to evict you. We loved each other."

For that matter, the burning in his chest told him he still did love her. More than he'd ever imagined. They just needed time to work out their problems.

"Note the past tense in that sentence." She straightened as if ready to leave.

And just like that, he totally understood why she'd been pissed off at him for refusing to get into confrontations. It felt like a slap in the face when you wanted to hash something out and the other person couldn't be bothered to have the conversation with you.

"What about our lapse in the desert?" Couldn't she see the need to think beyond what they wanted to what would be best if she conceived? "Don't you think it would be better to wait and see if we're going to be parents first?"

She shook her head and for the first time he saw a

hint of regret pass over her features. A woman dressed in a khaki jacket hurried out of a nearby office carrying a stack of files and an iced coffee, forcing Shannon to lower her voice again.

"Even if we are, that won't change the fact that we can't get along. We're not helping anyone in this equation by staying together in the short term, when we'll only walk away when all is said and done."

"But I'm done with leaving," he argued, surprised by how much he meant it. Surprised by how much fighting for her meant to him.

He knew she wasn't anything like his first wife. Shannon would never have given up on him so fast the way his ex had. Hell, she had already stuck around longer than Monica had.

"I won't become some sort of obligation just because you think it's the right thing to stick by me now." She stepped away from him and toward the exit sign pointing the way out. "That's not love, that's having a sense of responsibility."

The border agent who'd been working on their case appeared at the end of the hallway, his timing utter crap as far as Romero was concerned.

"That's not why I want you to stay." Frustration simmered and he fought the urge to clamp a hand on her shoulder and hold her there until he'd convinced her.

"I'm sorry, Romero." Her voice cracked over the words, but the knowledge that leaving hurt her, too, didn't buy him much consolation.

For a man perceived as a rock 'n' roll legend who had the world by the tail, Romero Jinks didn't feel very lucky at all.

IT HAD NEARLY KILLED HER, of course, but she did it.

Head held high, Shannon put on the performance of a lifetime as she strode out of the customs building. Ceily was waiting there, big sunglasses perched on top of her perfectly highlighted blond hair, a semi-smile stretched across pouty Botox-treated lips. Shannon waved, picking up her pace as she hurried to the parking lot, since she couldn't wait to get in the car and pour out her broken heart to the woman who'd been a friend as well as her professional rep for as long as Shannon had been in the business.

"Are you okay, honey?" Ceily asked as she moved closer to give her a hug. "Sounds like you've been through a total ordeal."

Shannon's eyes burned as she nodded, holding herself stiffly while Ceily squeezed her, since she couldn't risk losing a grip on her emotions out here where anyone could see. She didn't have as much practice at reining in her feelings off-screen, and she feared she had used up all possible reserves in her talk with Romero.

"You don't know the half of it," she whispered in her friend's ear before giving her a kiss on the cheek and stepping back. "I'll tell you about it on the way home."

Or, as it happened, on the way to Romero's home, which she now had to vacate with all possible haste, since she'd committed to being out this week.

Sliding into Ceily's Mercedes coupe, Shannon caught sight of a flashy red Ferrari pulling up nearby. Even if she hadn't spotted Romero jogging out to the vehicle with his duffel bag slung over his shoulder, she would have known his ride had arrived. The longtime drummer for Romero's band was one of Hollywood's hardest partyers and flashiest big spenders. No doubt Luther Zapo would help Romero forget all about his failed relationship.

Hurt gripped her all over again, but she wouldn't let it level her this time. Leaving would be for the best. She knew that now, after witnessing Romero struggle even to offer up another chance at cohabitation back there in the customs office. No more deceiving herself that he would suddenly turn into a man who could share more of himself with her than he already had.

Ceily pulled away from the curb, but not before Luther and Romero sped off in front of them. God only knew where they were going or where Romero would lay his head tonight.

Shannon might love the man to pieces, but if he couldn't return that love in full, she wouldn't stick around, crossing her fingers. No sir. She'd carve out a life of her own without seeking anyone else's approval.

Even if it shattered her heart into a million little pieces.

17

"THE SKY'S THE LIMIT tonight, bro."

Romero settled in the shotgun seat while his old friend steered his latest toy onto the interstate. Luther Zapo had been with him from the beginning, but just because they were bandmates didn't mean they always saw eye to eye. Luther's songwriting had petered out over the years, his focus more on touring and partying. But Romero had called him because the guy would never leave a buddy in the lurch.

And maybe Romero needed a night out to put thoughts of Shannon out of his head, at least for a little while.

"And I mean that literally, man," Luther continued, hammering the gas pedal as he took over the passing lane. "The sky's the limit, since I've got my plane on standby for you. You want to hit Vegas? It'd be just like old times."

Romero grinned at the memory of some of those trips. But they were just that—memories. He hadn't been to Vegas in years. At first, he'd avoided the city that had been the setting for his train wreck of a marriage. But lately, he'd either been on tour or with Shannon.

"I don't know, Zap." Romero couldn't picture himself in Sin City tonight. For one thing, he might fall asleep after the first Alabama Slammer. For another, he'd probably be so freaking preoccupied with Shannon that he would be zero fun.

"Okay, then we hit the bars closer to home. There's a new strip club north of the city and the girls are smoking hot. A couple of lap dances and you'll be good as new, bro." Zapo cranked up the stereo for a classic Doors tune.

Until Romero turned the volume back down.

"You know, things aren't over with me and Shannon." Not by a long shot. The patrol station at the border hadn't been a good place to discuss her moving or a possible pregnancy, not to mention the incredible fireworks between them back there in that desert. But he planned to talk to her about it in detail after he'd given her time to get home and clean up. Maybe catch up on sleep.

All of which only made him think about her showering and lying in bed, which tempted him to go back to their house right now.

"That's not what I read online, dude." Zapo frowned as he adjusted his rearview mirror. "What kinds of cars do the cops drive down here, anyway?"

Romero squeezed his temples and wondered why he didn't have any normal friends who did stuff like watch football games on the big-screen TVs in bars or play poker at each other's houses. But he'd gone from his conservative father's domain to a hard-partying lifestyle, with nothing in between—until Shannon.

She was the best blend of stay-at-home and fun. Totally entertaining, yet not wild enough to end up in jail. The way Zapo would if he didn't bring down the speed in the Ferrari.

"I don't know, Zap. I think you'd better drop me off at my house."

"Your house? You mean where Shannon's staying?" He pulled into the center lane, but the Ferrari didn't exactly blend in. Tugging his shades off, he threw them on the dashboard in a comical attempt to look like an upstanding citizen. "Shit, man. Why didn't you just drive home with her if you were only going to end up spending the night with her, anyhow?"

Because she hadn't invited him. Because it hadn't been the right time to convince her he wanted another chance to make it work with her. Because he hadn't realized just how much he needed to be with her until he'd slid into Zap's passenger seat and remembered what had driven him to seek Shannon out in the first place.

He'd loved that movie she made about a groupie-turned-muse for a weathered rock star. Romero had half fallen in love with her image on-screen, but maybe he'd been seeing himself in the hero's shoes, too. He might want to make music until he was a hundred and ten, but that didn't mean he had to live on the road and hit the strip clubs.

Maybe he'd wanted to dial down his rowdy lifestyle all along, and it had just taken him this long to see a way how to do that and not end up with the monotonous existence of his clan back home.

He could make it work. And now he knew for damn certain that he wanted to.

"Actually, I think I'd better clean up and grab my guitar from the hotel before I see her." Romero straightened in his seat, already envisioning ways to make music without the constant touring. Songwriting was in his blood, and after the past twenty-four hours with Shannon, he could almost feel a song humming at the edges of his brain. "Just drop me off at the Beverly Wilshire and I'll owe you big-time."

More than Zap would ever know. It was thanks to him that Romero remembered why total freedom and independence weren't all they were cracked up to be. Being with Shannon was so much better than that. And for the first time in his whole effing life, sitting still sounded better than running.

"You're doing the right thing."

Ceily's words of assurance didn't soothe Shannon's heart any more than the mental pep talks she'd been giving herself the whole ride home. Shunning the media since her return from Mexico an hour ago, she'd closed herself up in the house she'd shared with Romero, and gotten to work packing her things for her trip to New York. For the move she needed to make, since she couldn't afford a mansion in the Hollywood Hills anymore.

Some of Romero's stuff was still here. A drum set that belonged to one of his friends. Snowshoes. A lot of damn hiking boots. Untangling their lives wouldn't be a simple task at any level.

Now, after feeding her deliriously happy-to-see-her dogs, and sharing a pizza with Ceily, Shannon was wound up and ready to pull an all-nighter on the packing. Because if she stopped and thought too hard about all she was leaving behind, she might feel those tears come back.

"I know." Sighing, Shannon tossed a stuffed penguin

from a trip to New Zealand with Romero into a half-empty box on her bed. "But just because I recognize that it's the smart thing to do doesn't mean I can flip the switch and not care about him anymore."

As the penguin fell into the box, the toy emitted its battery-activated honking sound, the noise that had made Romero buy it for her in the first place. She remembered how she'd tried to perfect her penguin mating call when they went out to view the birds in the wild. She'd never managed to attract any interest from the boy penguins, but she'd pulled a grin from her over-tired rocker after a hard stretch of his European tour.

Who would bring a smile to his face now when he needed to work less and play more?

"I don't mean about Romero," Ceily huffed as she slid out another drawer from Shannon's accessory dresser to pack the scarves and gloves. "I mean about the script. I hate to see you go to New York for that play, Shan. And this script about your mom sounds like just the thing to make critics take notice."

After her weekend lost in the desert, Shannon had come away with a need to do the *Baby Doll* film even though she still planned to meet with the New York producers next week. And she didn't just want to do the film because Romero had been right about the need to open herself up more on-screen. She also thought it might help her make peace with her feelings about her mother. As much as she might rail privately about the misconceptions about Bridget Leigh in the media, what had she ever done to counteract the generally held opinion? Had she let her mother's image remain tarnished because of some childish frustrations about her checking out and leaving Shannon to be raised by an aunt who saw her as little more than a source of cash?

Maybe so. But she didn't feel that way about her mother anymore and she would do everything in her power as an actress to paint Bridget Leigh's life in a way that was true to the big-scale drama and tragedy that had marked her time in Hollywood.

"I hope so." Shannon couldn't resist reaching for the chubby penguin again and rubbing the soft fur against her cheek. "I appreciate you fronting me a loan on my *Baby Doll* contract so I can rent a new place."

Not that she was overly enthused at the idea of being alone again in a cheap bungalow in Pasadena, but it had been generous of Ceily to offer to help her through the financial rough patch while she extricated herself from her old life. Once she and Romero sold this house…

Ah, it would be good and bad for too many reasons to count.

A shrill bark sounded at her feet, warning her that Costello, the smaller of her Pekingese-Chihuahua mixes, was envious of her attention to a stuffed animal. Silly dog. Setting the penguin back in the packing box full of belts and jewelry cases, Shannon bent to stroke his head just as the phone rang. For the tenth time that evening, Ceily picked it up to deal with whatever friend or media outlet wanted to hear about Shannon's desert ordeal.

"You poor baby," Shannon crooned, still missing Mary-Kate and Ashley, although she'd been thrilled to see Abbott and Costello happy and none the worse for the extra day she'd been away from them.

The first thing she'd done when she came back home was grab the dog food bag. After that, she'd sneaked a few minutes online to see how fast a pregnancy test would work, while Ceily ordered the pizza and dealt with a few of the more aggressive reporters outside. Apparently, the kits weren't effective until about six days after conception. Not that Shannon was superworried about a one-time slipup, but the timing was close to ideal if they'd been trying to have a baby.

With any luck, the indie filmmaker could start shooting fairly quickly on *Baby Doll* so Shannon could wrap up her part before she started to show. *If* she started to show. Otherwise, all this great planning she'd done for the tribute to her mom would be for naught.

"Someone's out front," Ceily shouted from the walk-in closet off the bedroom.

"Just tell them we're not receiving," Shannon yelled back. "Do you believe all the calls we've been getting? At this rate, I'll need a publicist. And wouldn't that be a slap in the face if I end up being best known for getting lost in the desert instead of some wonderful cinematic contribution?"

"Um…" Ceily stepped out of the closet, still gripping Shannon's cordless phone. "Actually, that wasn't your average tabloid-story hunter."

The agent slipped the phone back on its cradle near the bed, a peculiar expression on her face.

"Oh, God." Shannon's stomach dropped. "Don't tell me my star has risen to *People* magazine."

She looked terrible. She couldn't possibly let anyone inside the house—

"No." Ceily stepped into a pair of Shannon's Louboutin shoes, which Shannon had insisted be a down payment on the advance Ceily had floated her. "Romero's outside."

Shannon sank to the bed, her legs suddenly not as capable of supporting her as they had been a minute ago.

"I don't know if that's better or worse than *People* magazine."

Her whole body hummed with nervous energy, as if she'd just jabbed her finger into a light socket.

"Don't be silly." Ceily strode closer to kiss her on the cheek, the familiar scent of her custom-brewed perfume surrounding Shannon for a moment. "This is a good thing. I should really head home anyhow, but I'll call you in the morning to see if you want me to come back and help. Okay?"

Shannon nodded, feeling thoroughly abandoned. How could Ceily leave her to face the man who had so much power over her heart? The man who'd told her over and over again that he could give only so much of himself where relationships were concerned.

Ceily's high heels tapped a receding beat on the tile floors until she reached the door and turned.

"Hear him out, okay, Shannon? He might not express himself with big, sweeping gestures, but that doesn't mean the feelings aren't there."

The agent walked away before Shannon could argue. A clever tactic, since she realized she would have indeed argued with her friend. Which was all part of Ceily's point. Did Shannon put too much emphasis on battling her way to a happy ending?

Downstairs, she heard Romero's deep, delicious voice in the foyer, echoing up through the open-air gallery as he greeted Ceily. The rest of their exchange was too quiet to hear, but it only lasted a few moments before Romero's footsteps sounded on the curved staircase. Coming closer.

He rapped on the wall outside the bedroom they'd once shared. A warning knock to let her know he was on the way.

She gulped. Fought back a wave of...what? Happiness? Anxiety? Nostalgia? Her emotions were so knotted up, she didn't even know anymore.

"Hey, Shannon." Guitar slung over one shoulder, he stepped into the open doorway. His face was tanned from their time in the desert instead of pink like hers, she noted. He grinned at her as he lifted a hand to the door molding overhead and hung on it, as if determined to wait for an invitation before he charged into his old bedroom. "I'm home."

18

BEFORE ANY BIG GIG, Romero ran through the performance in minute detail, making sure everything from the sound and the lights to the security and special effects were in good working order.

He'd wanted to approach his reunion with Shannon the same way in order to make sure this meeting ended how he wanted. Unfortunately, he'd rushed over here as soon as he'd showered and changed, his head full of a half-written song and his heart full with…well, *her.*

"What are you doing here?" Shannon sat on the bed with her arms crossed, her whole posture defensive.

Which was strange, since she usually took a more offensive approach. Her normal M.O. ran to hands gesticulating, fingers pointing, body language in his face and close up. The difference worried him. He'd planned his remarks to address the concerns of his dramatic, passionate ex. What if he'd miscalculated?

Worse, what if her more conservative response meant she didn't care? He'd never realized her more aggressive moods at least indicated that she wanted to be with him. That she wanted to work things out between them.

"Can't I stop by the house?" He pried his fingers off

the doorjamb and entered the room, determined to lay out his hopes for a future together without the conversation turning into a confrontation. Or without making himself comfortable on that bed beside her to convince her they belonged together.

In his dry run of this conversation, he'd poured his heart into a declaration she deserved to hear. But in real life, he'd never tossed off an "I love you" with any more feeling than most people gave to a phrase like "right back at you." He'd said it as an endearment, not a pledge of eternal devotion.

But all that was about to change.

"It was *you* who left to begin with. I guess I didn't expect to see you back until I'd gone." Rising to her feet, Shannon turned to the nightstand on her side of the bed and opened a drawer, apparently emptying the contents into the box beside her.

Just seeing her surrounded by so much corrugated cardboard and packing paper twisted his heart. Even Abbott and Costello had their luggage packed and sitting by the door—brown cloth cases printed with ivory-colored bones.

Choosing not to engage in the contentious conversational opening she'd given him, Romero whistled for the dogs and sat down on the bed to scratch them. Neither of the boys were supposed to be on the mattress, but when the canines spied Romero they immediately broke that rule, highlighting his inability to discipline them. Shannon said nothing, continuing to stack some books and DVDs into the box.

She looked incredible. Makeup free and with her hair loose, she reminded him of the stripped-down way she'd dressed while trekking around the Sonoran Desert with him. She wore a light blue tank top that made her eyes seem all the more aqua. A little white cotton sweater with big, crocheted holes covered the tank top, but not enough that he couldn't see plenty of bare skin.

"Ceily told me you're going to do the movie." He spied a stuffed penguin on the bed near Costello and, recognizing a long-ago souvenir, picked it up. Ceily had also asked him about taking on a docudrama himself, but Shannon was the film star in this relationship. He'd think about consulting, but he had no desire for the big screen.

"I decided I'm not ready to go to New York yet." She banged the nightstand drawer open and shut again, then straightened. "Actually, that's not true. I'm still meeting with the producers next week to talk. But what you said in the desert about me not always putting myself forward in my movies really hit home. I want the chance to change that before I give up on Hollywood."

A prickle of worry ran up the back of his neck.

"I didn't mean to suggest you weren't a fantastic actress. The whole reason I went out of my way to meet you was because—"

"Because of my groupie movie. I know. I remember." She gave a lopsided grin that didn't strike him as overly happy. "But that was an understated part—something I've been drawn to as an actress, perhaps because I've shied away from larger-than-life characters like my mother played. Like my mother *was*."

"I think the film will open a lot of doors for you." He'd never critiqued her professional choices, respecting the kind of career she'd chosen for herself. But since he knew the level of her talents, he couldn't deny taking pleasure in seeing her agree to a more risky piece. "You deserve the kind of critical recognition this will bring your way."

"There aren't too many people in the industry who would agree with that assessment, since as of now, I'm on the verge of being broke and bankrupt in this field." She tapped the framed movie poster from a big teen flick she'd done after she'd been declared an emancipated minor by the courts. "My earnings haven't equaled what I got for *Prom Girl's Revenge* in a long time."

"*Baby Doll* will wipe *Prom Girl* off the map." He walked closer to the poster. To her. "I brought back the Vera Wang."

He might have blown a chance to say something sensitive there, but his dress rehearsal hadn't accounted for the tangent about her movie.

"You what?" She spun to face him, her tempting body within easy touching distance as she stared up at him with a new light in her eyes.

"The recovery company will tow the car to the States tomorrow, but they went ahead and sent someone out to pick up the rest of our bags. Nothing was taken that I noticed, but I only looked in your suitcase long enough to see that your bridesmaid's dress was there."

"That's great." She nodded and gave him the obligatory smile. "Thank you. But I'd really better get back to packing, so if that's all…"

Crap.

His plans for this reunion weren't working out one bit if she was already prepared to give him the boot. He hadn't said half of what needed saying.

Maybe the time had come to scrap the rehearsed stuff and go with his gut.

"No." He reached out to her, stroking his hands down her arms because he couldn't stop himself anymore. "I'm not ready to leave. I came here to ask for a second chance."

THE MAN DIDN'T FIGHT FAIR.

Not only did he never raise his voice, he also used the most persuasive weapon in his arsenal—the power of touch. Shannon forced herself not to melt at his feet, and stepped back, needing to have this conversation with a clear head.

"Why?" Folding her arms across a *far* too responsive body, she stared him down. "Why should we try this again when we've failed so miserably and publicly in the past?"

She wasn't proud of the big fight that had placed his belongings in neat rows of packing boxes outside their house. Thanks to jerks like Selby, half the country had seen telling pictures of their argument's aftermath.

Romero stalked around the bedroom, dodging boxes and taking in the other movie posters on the walls. She'd worried a little at first that she'd appear way too narcissistic for hanging them, but pats on the back didn't come easy or often in her industry, and she'd appreciated the reminders that she had managed to forge a living in a supercompetitive field.

"Because I'm ready to fight for you now." He halted, pulling his gaze from a promo still of her costars in a film where she'd played a teen detective. "I wasn't ready last year or even last week. I thought family life would suffocate me the way I watched it suffocate my dad. He stifled his dream of going to law school in order to take over the family business, a business he never really even liked. Over the years, the dinner table conversation deteriorated to what kinds of brake pads and fuel filters the store should stock. It was like all his passions sort of died because he hadn't done what he really wanted to."

Shannon listened, curious. She'd never heard Romero talk much about his father, but maybe she hadn't thought it odd. Her own mother died so young, and Shannon had never known her dad. Didn't even know his name. She didn't have a good comparison to know how much people *should* talk about their parents.

"And then, later, they gave my oldest sister props for coming home to have kids and work at the auto-parts store, after a turn at Juilliard."

"You sister went to Juilliard?" Shannon wondered why she'd never heard about that before. Maybe she'd given up asking Romero about his family too easily, since he hadn't liked to talk about them.

"She's got a gift. A talent that, honest to God, makes my act sound like some suburban garage band." He shook his head. "I couldn't believe nobody else in the family encouraged her to follow her dream. It seemed so wrong. And they gave me hell for telling her to try her luck. I told her I'd move to New York if she needed a place to stay or if she wanted company."

"That was sweet of you." Shannon wondered what it would have been like to have a supportive brother to lean on.

"Yeah, well, no one else thought so. But I didn't

want to ever become so attached to the idea of family that I gave up my own dreams." He shrugged. "My dad's Family First motto became this brainwashing mantra I saw myself running away from because life on the road was everything that a family couldn't be."

She smiled. "Sex, drugs and rock 'n' roll?"

"Freedom. Art. Discovery. But keep that on the down low from the media, okay? It'd ruin my bad-boy rep."

He was still circling the room, and Shannon watched him, trying to absorb the message behind the words he'd finally chosen to share with her, after she'd fought for so long to understand what made him tick.

"But you've never had much in common with your family. What makes you think they'd ever influence your decisions now, after a lifetime of blazing your own path? Did you think you'd suddenly turn into an iron-fisted patriarch if you settled down with someone?"

"No." He paused for a long moment. "But I guess being with you made me afraid that all I've fought for—independence, freedom, the bohemian life—really doesn't amount to jack shit in the end if there's no one to share it with. Maybe I didn't want to admit the old man was right and it's possible to have that family dream on my own terms—our terms, Shannon. The truth is, it really *is* more important to have someone to come home to than to visit another exotic city."

The admission touched her like a warm bolt to her chest, filling her with new hope.

"But you wouldn't have found me without taking the path through every exotic city imaginable." She took a step closer to him. "You followed your dream then and you continue to follow your dreams now. Oh, and you managed to share your joy in life with millions of people around the globe on the way."

Romero lifted a dark eyebrow in an expression she remembered from one of his earliest album covers. It was a face fans had fallen in love with, but they didn't know the real man beneath the hot exterior. The emotional, complex and warmhearted man who sounded as if he was honestly thinking about how to have a future with her.

"I don't believe the old man will ever see it that way. In fact, even if we had a baby tomorrow, I'm sure I'd hear no end of it that I don't have five more kids because I couldn't settle my butt down."

"Five?" She swallowed hard. "Uh, I hate to disappoint you, but I won't even know if we're a go for one, since I have to wait until later in my cycle for a pregnancy test to be accurate." Her jaw clenched at the disappointment etched in his dark eyes. "I'm sorry I didn't tell you that bit of news as soon as you walked in."

Romero wrapped her in his arms too tightly for her to say any more than that. He squeezed her close for a moment before relaxing his hold, his hands smoothing down her back while he kissed her shoulder.

"It's good either way, okay? I promise, we can work it out no matter what happens. I'd love to have a family with you because it finally feels so right to me, but more than anything, I just want to be with you." He pulled back to look into her eyes. "I love you, Shannon."

She was grateful he'd kept a hold on her arms or she might have swooned like a teenage Elvis fan. He'd said the words to her before, but never like this. Never like he meant it with every fiber of his being. Her pulse picked up speed as a rush of blood warmed her insides.

"Wow." It wasn't much of a response, but then she was fairly breathless. "Really?"

Okay, maybe she was fishing for more of that "love" admission, but she figured she'd waited long enough to hear those words that she deserved to savor every wonderful facet of them.

"I swear to you. It's the real thing." He led her to the bed and, clearing away boxes, sat her down. "It about tore my heart out to think we might really be through today. I wrote a song about you after you left me at the border."

Curling her feet beneath her, she settled against the piles of pillows near the headboard and watched him pick up his guitar.

It had been a long time since he'd shared this part of himself with her. She felt fortunate to be an audience of one for this megatalented man.

"Do I get to hear it?"

"It's not finished." He ducked under the guitar strap, adjusting his favorite old acoustic at his hip. His fingers already danced along the strings, warming up. Tuning. Testing. All a matter of seconds for a man who had lived and breathed guitar his entire adult life.

"But I get to hear a little?" Anticipation warmed her.

He nodded and launched into a series of chords, the music swelling, filling the room. He hummed a few notes that she knew meant he'd just laid in the melody in those parts, then sang some key lyrics about broken promises giving way to new dreams.

"That first night together, turned into forever. Your love put a spell on me…."

The tune was gorgeous. Shannon could see a hit song in the making. But more important, she could hear the way Romero felt about her in the lines. Between the lines. In the quiet power of his voice.

By the time he was done, she had to swipe a tear from her eye.

"I can't believe—" She gulped back another happy tear, touched more than she could say. "That was so beautiful."

He grinned as he tugged the guitar up and off, setting it in a corner of the room before he joined her on the bed.

"I was already thinking it up on the way home after we left the border." He dropped an arm around her and drew her against him until her head rested on his chest. She could hear the reassuring beat of his heart right beneath her ear.

"You sped off in Zapo's Ferrari like a bat out of hell."

"That was him driving, not me. And he thought he could cheer me up with bar hopping or VIP rooms at some new strip club, but that sounded so lame to my ears that I knew I wasn't walking out of the desert the same guy who'd walked in."

Shannon ran her hand up his arm, feeling the hard strength of his muscles beneath the thin silk of his dress shirt. Oh, heaven help her, she loved this man.

"We did have a pretty good time in spite of the mountain lion, didn't we?"

"And the sleazebag following our every move."

"And the fact that I left behind Vera Wang." She glanced up at him, needing that warm connection of his gaze on hers.

His eyes darkened and she could tell a kiss was coming. She couldn't wait.

"Guess it's true what they say about love conquering all." His mouth brushed hers in a kiss that sent her senses reeling in two seconds flat.

She wrapped her arms around his neck to drag him closer, wanting nothing so much as to lose herself in this man. This moment.

The dogs' nails clicked on the tiles before they bounded up on the bed, their wiggly bodies bumping up against them as if they wanted to get in on the happiness and love radiating from the two of them. A thought that reminded her…

"I love you, too, Romero." She confessed the secret she'd been so desperate to hold back from him when he'd first walked in here today. "For real. For always."

"I'm going to make up for every time I've walked away from you when you were upset. I promise."

"I appreciate that." She never wanted to hear the sound of tires squealing on the driveway again. "But I know sometimes it's been for the best. We don't always need to create a big drama over minor stuff. And we definitely don't need to move to Iowa."

"You see why I love you so much?" He stroked his fingers over her cheek and brushed her hair away from her face.

"I don't need a family so badly that I have to go out and adopt all your sisters, although I think if we spend a little time there together we can show the Jinks clan that you can have a family even while you're on the move. Kids don't have to mean the end of freedom or travel or following your dreams."

"What if my mom tries to brainwash you with the 'family first' bit? She'll be sending you housing prices for big, glitzy ranches back in Iowa."

"Then I'll introduce her to the lure of Rodeo Drive shopping and she'll know why Iowa just isn't a possibility for me." When Costello nudged her leg again, she got another idea. "Or maybe I'll bring the dogs out to meet her next time and the boys' matching swim trunks will send the subtle message that I belong with the rest of the wing nuts in the great state of California."

"You wicked woman, you." He grinned.

She rocked her hips against his and licked her lips, ready to begin her new life with Romero doing what they did best.

"You don't know the half of it, superstar." She reached for the first button on her shirt and popped it open. "But stick around and you'll find out."

Epilogue

Nine months later

HE DID STICK AROUND, too.

Romero couldn't help but take a small amount of pride in that, because he hadn't sat still anywhere for nine months straight since he was stuck in high school, waiting for his eighteenth birthday. And this time wasn't even because Shannon had come up pregnant, since she'd taken a test a week after they returned home that proved negative.

No, Romero had moved back into the house with Shannon, Abbott and Costello because he belonged there. No more running. No more touring, at least for now. He was writing songs for other performers—up-and-coming acts and a few big names—and he'd never been more fulfilled creatively. It seemed strange that his life had fallen so perfectly into place because of a hit-and-run in a Mexican desert, but the experience had been a much-needed kick in the ass to make him appreciate what he'd been about to lose.

Even now, his brain rebelled at just the thought of being without the incredible woman in the seat beside him.

"I'm so nervous." Shannon sat next to him in the

back of the limousine, her nails lodged in his thigh as they circled the theater where *Baby Doll* was premiering tonight.

"You don't have anything to be nervous about, sweetheart." He leaned over to kiss her cheek, her perfectly made-up features the result of hours' worth of primping by a team she'd chosen to ensure a good showing on the red carpet.

Personally, he thought she looked the hottest when she was wearing nothing but one of his T-shirts, but as a performer himself, he appreciated the level of showmanship Shannon brought to her big night.

"Sure I don't." She turned to frown at him before her blue eyes shot back to the scenery out the window—the camera crews and an A-list audience all wanting to know why there was so much buzz for an indie movie. "I've only got a comeback at stake on my ability to stay upright through a sea of cameras while perched on the narrowest stilettos I've ever worn. Not to mention the pins that fell out of my hair when I opened the window for some fresh air. What if the whole thing topples?" She patted her updo with hands that shook ever so slightly.

Romero assessed the sleekly coiffed hair that looked far too well behaved to stray from its confines, knowing his soon-to-be wife was really stressing about the critics' reception of the first film she'd invested a huge amount of herself in. Not just her art. Not her perfectly trained acting ability. But her *self.*

Wrapping an arm lightly around her shoulders, he ran his thumb beneath the strap of a silk cocktail dress with a floating layer of pale aqua over a sheath of deep marine blue. A color scheme he was intimately familiar with, since her choice of dress had been a household topic for weeks.

Between their discussions of everything, nothing, and solving the world's problems over coffee and croissants, it seemed like old times.

"Honestly, I don't think your hair will fall without your help, but if it were me, I'd take it all down and attend this shindig with a little more rock 'n' roll attitude." He shrugged to make sure she didn't take him superseriously, since he'd never seen her so tightly wound. "Not that I know a lot about these things."

"Rock 'n' roll?" She patted her hair again, her hand nudging one of her dangling gold-and-sapphire earrings until it swung like a hyperactive pendulum.

"Yeah. Free. Making your own rules." He slipped his hand just a little deeper into her dress, grateful for the tinted glass that ensured no one could see what they were doing even though the car attracted plenty of attention on this stretch of Hollywood Boulevard.

A slow shiver coasted over her as his finger dipped into the confines of her strapless bra.

"You wicked man." Her eyes closed. "You're trying to relax me."

"Hell, Shannon, I'm trying to seduce you." He reached across her to slide his other hand up her skirt just a few inches. "You could step out onto that carpet with flushed cheeks and tousled hair as if you'd just gotten it on in the back of a limo. It'd make a great style statement."

She laughed, a rich, throaty sound that was miles away from her tight-lipped commentary earlier on this ride. He wanted her to have fun tonight. To enjoy every moment of recognition soon to be heaped on her.

"And since when do I take fashion tips from a rock 'n' roll legend?" She scooted closer on the bench seat, giving his hand better access beneath the hem of her dress.

He palmed her thigh and wondered how far he could take this. She sure had allowed herself to live a little more on the edge since their reunion after returning from Mexico. Not only had she taken the risky part of her mother in an edgy, independent film, she'd also started throwing some low-key dinners for fellow cast members the way she used to for the neighbors, finally allowing people from her work world to see what she was like at home. With her hair down.

On top of that, she'd flown his mother out to L.A. to show her the town—something Romero had never thought his conservative father would go for. But somehow Shannon had won him over with a DVD library of all of Bridget Leigh's films. Shannon seemed to enjoy making some inroads with his close-knit kin, yet, God love her, she never tried to force Romero into any extra Iowa trips.

"Since you became the muse of this rock 'n' roll legend." He bent to place a kiss just above the strands of gold chains around her neck. "You can let me play Svengali with you every now and then, right?"

She laughed at the reminder of a video they'd shot together a few weeks ago, an elaborate production for a stand-alone single he was bringing to market next month. He didn't plan to make another full-on album anytime soon, but since the song was one of several he'd written about his newfound happiness after so many years as a rolling stone, he thought it deserved to be shared.

And Shannon had had a blast playing the young muse to his worldly persona in the video—their nod to the film of hers that first brought them together.

"Not a chance." Still, she pulled a few more pins out of her hair and let the long strands slither out of their elaborate knot. "But maybe I can loosen up just a little for this event. It's my time to shine. I might as well be the real me."

Oh, yeah.

He whistled appreciatively as she transformed from coolly regal to California girl.

"Besides…" she shook out her hair and set the pins aside "…you wrote the song that's made this movie so talked-about even before it came out. I owe you for that."

Romero released her thigh to tuck a section of her hair behind her ear so an earring showed.

"You can take full credit for that song, babe." He still couldn't believe the wellspring of creativity that had bubbled up inside him because of her. Because of loving her.

He'd never been so prolific in his life.

"You wrote it," she protested. "It was your lyrics that made it go to number one."

"Some would say it's that new boy band that made it go to number one." Still, he appreciated her ardent belief in him, her absolute faith. And, yeah, it was kind of cool that top-ranked artists vied for the chance to perform a Romero Jinks tune.

He brushed another kiss on her shoulder as the limo driver got in the line to drop them off for the premiere.

"They're not the half of it," Shannon insisted. "I just hope the movie lives up to the hype built by your song."

Romero eased his hand out from under the strap of her dress.

"Hey, no more talk like that or I'll have to go back to the plan where I send you out there with very flushed cheeks."

She blushed on cue, but grinned, too. "Don't you get me all flustered when I have to talk to those camera crews."

Romero double-checked out his window, even though he knew Steve Selby wouldn't be there. The dirtball photographer had moved to New York to harass stars on the other coast after his tabloid employer heard about the lawsuit Romero had considered at one point.

"You're sexiest when you're flustered," he assured her, surprised how excited he was for her big night. For her.

Damn but he was proud.

"Is that right?" She straightened in her seat as she realized they were almost at the drop-off point. "How would you like it if I told you exactly how I'm going to undress you on this very seat on our way home to-night?"

Romero's mouth went dry at the thought. Right as the limo moved forward toward the greeters in front of the red carpet leading into the theater.

"See?" She stroked his thigh with her fingernails in the last second before the limo door opened. "It makes it tough to think straight, doesn't it?"

Before she could slide across the seat and step out into the eager crowd, Romero held her back in the shadows of the car.

"You're a wild woman, Shannon Leigh." And he loved her more than anything.

She cradled his face in her hand, her expression intense. Focused. Passionate.

"Thank you for reminding me."

He kissed her—hard and fast—before he released her to greet her fans. The squeals in the crowd were music to his ears as he watched her step into the spotlight she deserved.

They'd decided to wait on kids a little longer after the close call. They had some travel plans in front of them, after all. Their wedding was in four more weeks on a beach in Hawaii, since Shannon had said he couldn't run away from her—but he could always run away *with* her.

One of many reasons he fell more in love with her every damn day.

* * * * *

Harlequin is 60 years old,
and Harlequin Blaze is celebrating!
After all, a lot can happen in 60 years,
or 60 minutes…or 60 seconds!
Find out what's going down in
Blaze's heart-stopping new miniseries,
FROM 0 TO 60!
Getting from "Hello" to "How was it?"
can happen fast….

Here's a sneak peek of the first book,
A LONG, HARD RIDE
by Alison Kent.
Available March 2009.

"IS THAT FOR ME?" Trey asked.

Cardin Worth cocked her head to the side and considered how much better the day already seemed. "Good morning to you, too."

When she didn't hold out the second cup of coffee for him to take, he came closer. She sipped from her heavy white mug, hiding her grin and her giddy rush of nerves behind it.

But when he stopped in front of her, she made the mistake of lowering her gaze from his face to the exposed strip of his chest. It was either give him his cup of coffee or bury her nose against him and breathe in. She remembered so clearly how he smelled. How he tasted.

She gave him his coffee.

After taking a quick gulp, he smiled and said, "Good morning, Cardin. I hope the floor wasn't too hard for you."

The hardness of the floor hadn't been the problem. She shook her head. "Are you kidding? I slept like a baby, swaddled in my sleeping bag."

"In my sleeping bag, you mean."

If he wanted to get technical, yeah. "Thanks for the

loaner. It made sleeping on the floor almost bearable." As had the warmth of his spooned body, she thought, then quickly changed the subject. "I saw you have a loaf of bread and some eggs. Would you like me to cook breakfast?"

He lowered his coffee mug slowly, his gaze as warm as the sun on her shoulders, as the ceramic heating her hands. "I didn't bring you out here to wait on me."

"You didn't bring me out here at all. I volunteered to come."

"To help me get ready for the race. Not to serve me."

"It's just breakfast, Trey. And coffee." Even if last night it had been more. Even if the way he was looking at her made her want to climb back into that sleeping bag. "I work much better when my stomach's not growling. I thought it might be the same for you."

"It is, but I'll cook. You made the coffee."

"That's because I can't work at all without caffeine."

"If I'd known that, I would've put on a pot as soon as I got up."

"What time *did* you get up?" Judging by the sun's position, she swore it couldn't be any later than seven now. And, yeah, they'd agreed to start working at six.

"Maybe four?" he guessed, giving her a lazy smile.

"But it was almost two…" She let the sentence dangle, finishing the thought privately. She was quite sure he knew exactly what time they'd finally fallen asleep after he'd made love to her.

The question facing her now was where did this relationship—if you could even call it *that*—go from here?

* * * * *

*Cardin and Trey are about to find
out that great sex is only the beginning....
Don't miss the fireworks!*

Get ready for
A LONG, HARD RIDE
by Alison Kent.
Available March 2009,
wherever Blaze books are sold.

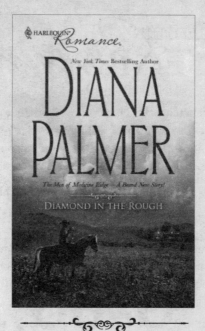

DIAMOND IN THE ROUGH

John Callister is a millionaire rancher, yet when he meets lovely Sassy Peale and she thinks he's a cowboy, he goes along with her misconception. He's had enough of gold diggers, and this is a chance to be valued for himself, not his money. But when Sassy finds out the truth, she feels John was merely playing with her. John will have to convince her that he's truly the man she fell in love with—a diamond in the rough.

THE MEN OF MEDICINE RIDGE—a brand-new miniseries set in the wilds of Montana!

Available April 2009 wherever you buy books.

www.eHarlequin.com

HRI7577

HARLEQUIN® *Romance*®

This February the Harlequin® Romance series
will feature six Diamond Brides stories featuring
diamond proposals and gorgeous grooms.

Share your dream wedding proposal and you could WIN!

The most romantic entry will win a diamond
necklace and will inspire a proposal in one of
our upcoming Diamond Grooms books in 2010.

In 100 words or less, tell us the most romantic
way that you dream of being proposed to.

For more information, and to enter
the Diamond Brides Proposal contest, please visit
www.DiamondBridesProposal.com

Or mail your entry to us at:

IN THE U.S.: 3010 Walden Ave., P.O. Box 9069, Buffalo, NY 14269-9069
IN CANADA: 225 Duncan Mill Road, Don Mills, ON M3B 3K9

The Inside Romance newsletter has a NEW look for the new year!

Same great content, brand-new look!

The Inside Romance newsletter is a FREE quarterly newsletter highlighting our upcoming series releases and promotions!

Click on the Inside Romance link on the front page of **www.eHarlequin.com** or e-mail us at insideromance@harlequin.ca to sign up to receive your FREE newsletter today!

You can also subscribe by writing to us at: HARLEQUIN BOOKS Attention: Customer Service Department P.O. Box 9057, Buffalo, NY 14269-9057

Please allow 4-6 weeks for delivery of the first issue by mail.

HARLEQUIN® *Blaze*

COMING NEXT MONTH
Available February 10, 2009

#453 A LONG, HARD RIDE Alison Kent
From 0–60
All Cardin Worth wants is to put her broken family together again. And if that means seducing Trey Davis, her first love, well, a girl's got to do what a girl's got to do. Only, she never expected to enjoy it quite so much....

#454 UP CLOSE AND DANGEROUSLY SEXY Karen Anders
Drew Miller's mission: train a fellow agent's twin sister to replace her in a sting op. Expect the unexpected is his mantra, but he never anticipated that his trainee, Allie Carpenter, would be teaching him a thing or twelve in the bedroom!

#455 ONCE AN OUTLAW Debbi Rawlins
Stolen from Time, Bk. 1
Sam Watkins has a past he's trying to forget. Reese Winslow is desperate to remember a way home. Caught in the Old West, they share an intensely passionate affair that has them joining forces. But does that mean they'll be together forever?

#456 STILL IRRESISTIBLE Dawn Atkins
Years ago Callie Cummings and Declan O'Neill had an unforgettable fling. And now she's back in town. He's still tempting, still irresistible, and she can't get images of him and tangled sheets out of her mind. The only solution? An unforgettable fling, round two.

#457 ALWAYS READY Joanne Rock
Uniformly Hot!
Lieutenant Damon Craig has always tried to live up to the Coast Guard motto: Always Ready. But when sexy sociologist Lacey Sutherland stumbles into a stakeout, alerting his suspects—and his libido—Damon knows he doesn't stand a chance....

#458 BODY CHECK Elle Kennedy
When sexually frustrated professor Hayden Houston meets hot hockey star Brody Croft in a bar, she's ready for a one-night stand. But can Brody convince Hayden that he's good for more than just a body check?

www.eHarlequin.com

HBCNMBPA0209

You're invited to join our Tell Harlequin Reader Panel!

By joining our new reader panel you will:

- Receive Harlequin® books—they are FREE and yours to keep with no obligation to purchase anything!
- Participate in fun online surveys
- Exchange opinions and ideas with women just like you
- Have a say in our new book ideas and help us publish the best in women's fiction

In addition, you will have a chance to win great prizes and receive special gifts! See Web site for details. Some conditions apply. Space is limited.

To join, visit us at

www.TellHarlequin.com.

Tell HARLEQUIN

REQUEST YOUR FREE BOOKS!

2 FREE NOVELS
PLUS 2
FREE GIFTS!

HARLEQUIN®

Blaze™

Red-hot reads!

HB08R